DON'T SPEAK

RAEANN CARTER

This is a work of fiction. Names, characters, places, and incidents are products of the author's imagination or are used fictitiously and are not to be construed as real. Any resemblance to actual events, locations, organizations, or persons, living or dead, is entirely coincidental.

World Castle Publishing, LLC
Pensacola, Florida
Copyright © RaeAnn Carter 2019
Paperback ISBN: 9781950890682
eBook ISBN: 9781950890699
First Edition World Castle Publishing, LLC, September 30, 2019
http://www.worldcastlepublishing.com
Cover: Karen Fuller
Editor: Maxine Bringenberg

CHAPTER 1
WELCOME HOME

My hands trembled, and I could feel my pulse vibrating throughout my entire body as I sat at the police station, still fearing for my life. The events I had just survived were mind boggling and left me in a state of terror. I took a few more sips of coffee while trying to wrap my head around what had just happened before the sheriff looked at me and said, "Leah, I need you to try to relax and start at the beginning. We need a detailed statement from you, okay?" It was hard for me to process anything he was saying. I had a million things going through my mind all at once.

"Have you found him?" I asked in a state of panic, "Please tell me you have him!"

"We are doing everything we can, Leah. I promise you are safe right now, and I'm going to make sure you stay safe until we find him. But right now I need you to start at the beginning and tell me everything that happened. Can you do that for me?"

"I need a cigarette," I stated.

The sheriff reached into the pocket of his leather jacket

and pulled out a pack of Marlboro Reds. "Here you go." He tossed them to me.

I removed a cigarette from the half empty pack and put it to my lips. He struck a lighter and held the flame up for me. I had not smoked since my senior year in high school, but I was desperate to calm my nerves. I took one drag from the cigarette before reliving my terror. As I began to give my statement to him, my mind became flooded with vivid flashbacks....

***

I had come to Rockwood County two years ago to attend college. My dream was to become a psychologist, and I had devoted my life to the study of human behavior. Lincoln University was well known for its outstanding psychology department, so naturally, I was overjoyed when I discovered I was granted a scholarship to attend.

I grew up in a small country town that I had longed to escape my entire life. There were no opportunities there unless I wanted to work at the same local factory everyone else in town worked at. I wanted more for my future. I didn't want to settle for factory work like everyone else that resided in the poverty-ridden town I called home.

When I first visited Rockwood, I immediately felt right at home. The quiet little county seemed to have plenty to offer a young woman like myself, with goals and tons of ambition. There was always something to do and plenty of new faces. Strangers smiled and were eager to greet a new face, which gave me a sense of comfort. As large as the area was, everybody seemed to know everybody. A real sense of community flooded the atmosphere. I didn't feel out of place because it reminded me of home, except it had much more to offer. I immediately knew this was a place where I could happily live out the next few years of my life.

During my first semester as an undergraduate at Lincoln, I met Trey Cooper, a tall, lanky gentleman with a crooked smile. I'll never forget the first time I saw him wandering the school hallway like a lost puppy on a mission. His wavy brown hair looked as if he'd overslept and didn't have a chance to comb it. There was just something about him that was perfectly imperfect.

Trey was devoted to computer science, and by looking at him, one would never believe he was a tech geek. He worked out religiously and held a jock persona — he was quite popular around campus. Underneath it all, he had a heart just as big as his dark brown eyes. The first time we spoke was quite embarrassing, but it was also the perfect icebreaker. I was still a fresh student at Lincoln and had no idea where I was going in such a large building. I misread my class schedule and wound up walking into the wrong classroom. The professor in that room was giving a lecture on computer technology when I came barging in, interrupting him. After clarifying that I was lost with at least thirty fellow students staring at me, Trey stood up and announced he would assist me to my class.

I fell madly in love with him the second I laid eyes on him, and it didn't take him long to return my emotions. We become serious about each other rather quickly. I'd often open up my textbook and find cute love notes he'd planted for me. As crazy as it may sound, I knew he was the one for me. He helped me loosen up and enjoy life more than I ever had while also respecting how dedicated I was to my studies. Trey would often sit with me between classes and help me study by calling out vocabulary words and such.

A year went by, and we were ready to take things to the next level. Due to Lincoln University's strict policies against sexual relations, we could have never roomed together in one of their dorms. I could barely share a kiss with him unless we were off campus, and even then, we had a strict 11:00 p.m. curfew. Can you imagine being twenty-one years old, as I was during this time, and having to sneak away just to kiss your boyfriend? We did not allow Lincoln's strict rules to stop us. Trey and I would meet after class every afternoon when we didn't have to work and leave campus to hang out until curfew. We did this for an entire year before growing increasingly sick of being controlled by ridiculous university laws. I came up with a plan to rent a place off campus together, and he was more than eager to follow through with the idea.

Both of us only held part-time jobs at a local hotdog stand during that time, so we knew we would need roommates in order to afford anything. If the wrong person were to discover either of us living with, or sleeping with, a member of the opposite sex, we could potentially face probation and possible suspension from school. The only people we could trust to room with us and remain silent were Trey's best friend, Dakota Johnson, and his girlfriend, Heather Baker.

Dakota was the quarterback of Lincoln's football team, and he had a complete frat boy way about him. He was as hardheaded as he was stubborn and prided himself on how much women loved him. He was a typical playboy and always used his good looks and charming ways to his advantage. Female professors admired his appearance, and male professors worshiped his athletic abilities. No matter how poorly he did with his academics, he aced every test. Fellow male students either envied him or hated him — there was no in between. Those that disliked him were most likely jealous, as it's easy to become when you stand next to a person like him. He made success look easy, and I imagine it wasn't pleasant for a young man to live in his shadow.

Regardless of what anyone's opinion of him may have been, he was a great guy. Anytime anyone needed help, Dakota could always be called upon. It was common for him to push everything on his agenda aside and assist someone with car trouble, carrying books, or opening doors. I met him through Trey, who had been his best friend since high school. The two of them actually both earned scholarships to attend Lincoln together. I grew attached to him and viewed him as an older brother.

His girlfriend Heather was also a psychology major, although she did not take her academics as seriously as I did. She preferred to spend her free time shopping. Her parents were financially well off and kept her supplied with credit cards, which Heather took full advantage of. She was devoted to keeping up with the latest fashion trends, and it was nothing for her to invest $500 on a new purse. She was one of the most free spirited individuals I ever had the pleasure of meeting. Always up for a new adventure and full of life,

Heather didn't sit around studying very often. If you didn't know her in person, it would've been easy to mistake her for a model fresh out of New York City. She definitely stood out compared to most other women in Rockwood, and she liked it that way.

I believe Dakota was so mesmerized by her because, unlike other women, she didn't bend over backward in an attempt to impress him. Heather knew her worth and could've had her choice in men, so there was no need for her to obsess over anyone. She and Dakota complemented each other well. He kept her more focused, and she challenged him in ways nobody else could. They were somewhat of a power couple — whatever quality one lacked the other had — and together, they were unstoppable.

Trey and I knew we could count on them to help with rent and utilities. Plus, they also had issues with Lincoln's strict rules and policies. They had both been placed on temporary probation the previous year when Dakota was caught in Heather's dorm room with no shirt on. Apparently, Heather's roommate at the time had a crush on Dakota, and out of spite, she reported them to the student service office. We hung out with them frequently and knew they would be on board with the idea of finding a place where we could live freely. Heather could afford rent with one of her credit cards alone, so together, the four of us could easily manage bills.

We did not have to search long before finding the perfect place, or so we thought. It was approximately twelve miles from campus and located at the very end of a narrow, secluded dirt road. From the dirt road, you could barely see the house due to the trees that lined the driveway and surrounded the property. It was like a small oasis hidden in the woods. The privacy was something we all longed for, and this house offered plenty.

There was just one downfall—the neighbors across the street from the driveway. They occupied the only other house on the road, and it looked more like an old abandoned barn than an actual home. The windows were broken, and the entire wooden structure appeared to be dry rotted. At one time, I imagine, it was probably a very beautiful house, but the years had not been kind to the property. The grass appeared as if no one had mowed it in years. The majority of it was dead, but the areas that remained were so overgrown a small child could've gotten lost in it. On the left side of the yard sat a pile of old tires that must have been there for a very long time. Moss and fungus had overgrown the majority of the tire pile, and I imagined it was most likely a snake's den. I knew there was something off about the inhabitants from day one.

***

"You're doing great, Leah; take a minute if you need to," the sheriff stated as I became lost in thought.

My gaze was drawn down toward the floor. "I'm fine," I responded. "Can I get a cup of water or something?"

"Sure, absolutely." The sheriff stood up, opened the door, and shouted, "Someone bring me a glass of water, please." Within a few seconds, an officer came in carrying a glass of water. "Thank you." The sheriff grabbed the water from the officer's hand and waited for him to exit the room before closing the door.

I wasn't entirely sure why I had requested water since I was not thirsty. Perhaps it was my anxiety getting the best of me, and I just needed something to do. Regardless, I took a sip before setting the cup down on the table in front of me.

The sheriff sat in silence for a moment before speaking up. "You said you noticed something off about the neighbors in the beginning. Can you explain what you mean by that?"

"It was a feeling I got." I paused for a moment. "They would just stare at us blankly; it was just strange." I continued with my statement as the events began to visually play through my mind once more....

***

I remember when we were moving things in, the neighbors would sit outside and just watch us go up and down the driveway as we unpacked the vehicles and reloaded them. There were four of them—a younger male, probably about my age; a middle-aged woman who always appeared to be holding a baby bundled up in a pink blanket on her lap; a small girl, probably no older than ten, I would guess; and an old woman. They all looked dirty like they had not bathed in months. They reminded me of old farmers or something from the 1950s, just lost in time and out of place. They would sit on their front porch and just stare at us—never blinking, never waving, just the emotionless stares. The only time I ever witnessed them move slightly was when they gently rocked back and forth in the rocking chairs they were seated in.

Judging by the ball of yarn that laid in her lap, the old woman always appeared like she was planning to knit something she'd never start. Her grey hair was wrapped in a bun ever so neatly on the top of her head. Her pale blue dress looked like it hadn't been washed in years.

The middle-aged woman sat on the far left and was always gently rocking her baby bundled up in that filthy pink blanket. She was a little heavyset, and I suspect she may have had a little back trouble by the way she slouched. Right next to her, on the floor of the wooden porch, sat the little girl, with her legs crossed. Wearing the same purple shirt and jean shorts every time I saw her, she didn't seem like an ordinary child. Most children her age have far too much energy to sit perfectly still like she did.

The young man could always be seen sitting on the staircase of the porch with his eyes closed. His filthy overalls and scuffed up boots suggested he was either ridden with poverty or a very hard worker. He was the only one that never stared because his eyes were always closed. He still directed his attention at us but kept his eyes closed, which was odd, to say the least.

I do not recall a time when I did not see all of them sitting outside on that porch, as if they never went inside. It didn't matter if it was eleven at night or seven in the morning; they were always sitting on that porch in the exact same spot as the day before, dressed in the same clothing, just staring.

I told Trey it was creepy the way they just stared at us, and while he certainly shared my feelings, he insisted they were just being typical nosey neighbors. I just assumed he was right. I guess it is normal to be curious when someone new is moving in near you. But the blankness on their faces, and the fact that they were always in the same position as the day before, made me feel uneasy.

One day, when we were moving the last of our things in, Dakota's tire popped at the foot of the driveway. We had driven over that very spot several times a day for a week and never had any issues, so it was odd to all of us when his tire popped so unexpectedly.

Dakota slammed the door on the truck with enough force to rattle the ground. "You've got tah be kidding me! I just got these tires!" He shouted. Of course, the neighbors were outside staring, but instead of ignoring them like we usually did, Trey tried to be sociable.

"Hey, how's it going? Looks like we have a flat."

They continued to stare blankly, completely ignoring Trey.

Heather nudged me to gain my attention. "Weirdoes," she whispered. They certainly were strange characters.

Trey turned his attention back to us and shrugged his shoulders to suggest he wasn't going to engage with them anymore.

Shortly after, Dakota became more frustrated when he realized he did not have his jack, which was needed to change the tire in his truck bed. Believing he must have misplaced it during the move, he commenced with cursing and stomping. Dakota never handled pressure very well and often became explosive over minor inconveniences. Trey, in an attempt to calm Dakota down, suggested using his car to run out and buy one.

"Man, that will take forever. We're losing daylight, and I have a lot of stuff to get moved in," Dakota announced in a daunting tone.

After stomping around in the road for a moment, Dakota decided to approach the neighbors. As he walked into their yard, asking if they had a jack he could use, the young man that had been sitting with his eyes closed all afternoon became aggressive. He stood up from the staircase and started yelling, "Stop looking! Stop looking!" We were all stunned, as this was the first time we had heard any of them say a word, and we certainly weren't expecting him to freak out like he did.

Dakota responded in a very confused tone. "Whoa, partner, calm down. I'm just trying to fix my tire."

Heather, who could sense the young man's hostile energy, immediately ran toward Dakota. She placed her hand on his chest and said, "Baby, come on, let's just go buy a jack, please."

The young man then yelled out at Heather, "Shh! Don't speak!" And that's when things escalated.

Dakota clenched his fist tightly as the look on his face completely changed into full-blown rage before he exclaimed, "What did you just say, punk?!"

About that time, the young man reached into his back pocket as if he were about to pull something out. My first thought was perhaps he was about to pull a gun on Dakota. Trey must have thought the same thing because he immediately spoke up. "Hey! Everybody, let's just calm down, okay?" He walked up and glanced at Dakota before turning his attention to the neighbors and continuing. "We don't want any trouble. My buddy here was not trying to disrespect you—he just thought you might have a jack."

Trey was holding his hands out, trying to appear peaceful, when the young man pulled a flashlight from his pocket. A sense of relief came over me when I saw it was something as harmless as a flashlight and not a gun. Strangely, the young man continued to turn the flashlight on, shining it toward Dakota, Trey, and Heather for a moment before he cut it off and placed it back into his pocket. We were taken aback by the strange action.

Before anybody could say anything else, a large middle-aged man in overalls opened the front door of the house and stepped out onto the porch, and exclaimed, "What the hell is going on out here?!"

We had never seen this person before. The man had a deep, forceful voice and a very intimidating manner. He wore no shirt under his filthy overalls and wore a straw hat full of holes. He definitely didn't blend in with the 21st-century atmosphere.

The young man immediately declared, with a faint tremble in his voice, "Th-they were speaking."

"Sir, we were just wondering if you guys had a jack. My buddy's tire just popped. We don't want any trouble, so we are just going to leave now, okay?" Trey stated.

The large man glared at Trey like he wanted to strangle him to death before responding. "A jack? Why didn't you just say so? I have one out back. Let me go grab it."

He smiled devilishly as he turned to walk toward his backyard. He paused to glare at the young man sitting on the staircase. With a snarl on his face, he told the boy he'd knock his teeth out if he ever woke him up yelling like that again.

I could tell the young man was terrified of him by the way he just timidly hung his head, never once opening his eyes. Perhaps even stranger than the young man keeping his eyes closed during the entire altercation were the mannerisms of the old lady, woman, and little girl. All three of them just sat there staring at us the entire time, never saying a single word. It was like nothing at all was happening.

After handing Trey the jack, the large man introduced himself. "I'm Roberson. I believe we're going to be neighbors?"

Trey passed the jack over to Dakota. "It appears that way. It's nice to meet you. I apologize for the minor altercation."

Dakota positioned the jack under the truck next to the dead tire. After loosening the bolts that held the tire to the axel, he gave the jack a few pumps with his foot, causing the side of the truck to rise in the air. He jerked the deflated tired off the axel, causing a loose bolt to fall off and roll underneath the truck. Heather hovered above him while he crawled under the vehicle to fish for the runaway bolt.

"Yeah, my son can get a little worked up around strangers. He means no harm," Roberson declared.

I walked a little closer to stand beside Trey during their conversation to remind him that we had a lot of work to do before nightfall. I couldn't help but notice how dirty Roberson's hands were. His fingernails were nearly black from the filth caked under them.

"Well, well, who is this fine young lady?" Roberson asked as he glared toward me like some sort of predator stalking its prey.

"Leah," I answered. "I'm Trey's girlfriend." I was sure to

grab onto Trey's arm to make myself appear unavailable to the strange creep.

Roberson stared at me for a moment as if something I said had angered him. He finally broke his silence. "Well, you must be the lucky Trey she's referring to?" He asked with a stiff glare.

"Yes, sir," Trey answered with a cheesy grin on his face.

Roberson immediately turned his attention toward Heather, who was still waiting for Dakota, who to find the runaway bolt. Roberson took a few steps toward her. "And who is this pretty girl?" Before she had a chance to answer, he added, "Good looking, and you seem to know your place. My type of woman."

I had no idea what he meant by that comment or what led him to make such a remark, but I knew Dakota wasn't going to appreciate it.

"That's my woman," Dakota immediately announced from under his vehicle with a hint of aggression.

Roberson appeared to be caught off guard by Dakota's lash out. "Well, excuse the piss out of me, boy!" Roberson exclaimed as he glared down toward Dakota.

Dakota was not the type to handle confrontation in a passive manner. He had too much pride to sit still and allow anyone to hit on Heather right in front of him. From underneath the truck, he mumbled, "Trust me, I'm not a boy. Just ask her."

Roberson crouched down to get closer to Dakota. "For someone that doesn't want any trouble, you sure have a smartass mouth on you, don'tcha boy?"

We heard a loud Ting! when Dakota dropped the crowbar on the ground. "And what are you going to do about it?" Dakota challenged.

Roberson slowly stood up and placed his boot on the jack that was holding the truck in place. "Well, I could just kick this really hard right now. I'd get my jack back, but the outcome may not go in your favor."

At that moment, Heather let out a shrill scream. "No! Please, sir!"

Knowing that if Roberson were to kick the jack out of place, the truck would fall onto Dakota and crush him, Trey sprinted over. "Hey. Come on now. He gets a little out of line sometimes, but there is no need to do anything crazy."

Roberson removed his foot from the jack and let out a deep chuckle. Dakota quickly rolled out from beneath the vehicle and exclaimed, "What the — what's wrong with you?!" He glared at Roberson as if he were trying to challenge him and threw his arms out to his sides.

"Relax," Roberson stated. "If I wanted to do something like that, I wouldn't have told you I was going to, now would I? I'm just messing with you, boy." He gave Dakota a nudge in a joking manner. "Now hurry up with that jack, so you kids can get back to your day, and I can get back to bed. And I'll take that old tire off of your hands and dispose of it for you."

We were all a little startled and didn't really know how to respond to the situation, so we just stood there in awkward silence. Dakota quickly changed the tire so that we could distance ourselves from Roberson as soon as possible. Roberson grabbed his jack and the old tire and walked away, never muttering another word.

As we were heading up the driveway to continue moving the remainder of our items into the house, I glanced in the passenger side mirror of Trey's car. Trey must have noticed me looking because he asked, "Are they still staring?" I nodded my head to confirm they were. "You know what's even stranger?" Trey asked.

"What?" I responded with a hint of curiosity.

"Dakota's tire had nails in it. I don't think he really paid attention, but I saw at least three nails on the back side on the tire."

"Why is that strange?" I asked.

"Well, how many times have we driven over that area this week while we have been moving in?" Trey responded.

"A lot, I guess. What's your point?"

"My point is it just seems weird. Almost like somebody recently set those nails there on purpose."

"So you think the neighbors purposely set nails down to pop one of our tires?" I asked.

"Maybe," Trey responded. "Let's not mention it to Dakota, though. We don't need him getting wired up again. On your way to class and work, just keep a look out to be safe."

CHAPTER 2
DON'T SPEAK AND DON'T LOOK!

I was awakened the following morning by the shrill sound of my alarm clock. "Beep! Beep! Beep!" I reached over and smacked the top button to shut it off. With sleep still in mind, I rolled over and shut my eyes.

"What the hell?!" I heard coming from outside the bedroom window. Dakota sounded pissed off about something. As much as I dreaded getting up at the moment, I couldn't return to sleep until I knew what his commotion was about. I stretched briefly, then got up and made my way outside to see what was causing his uproar.

To my surprise, Trey, Heather, and Dakota stood gathered around Dakota's vehicle, which had been vandalized. The windshield was smashed, and one of his taillights had been shattered. It was as if someone had beaten his car with a baseball bat or something.

"Damn bear!" He exclaimed in an attempt to place the blame on something.

Even though I highly doubted a bear was responsible for

the damage, I didn't attempt to argue with him. I instantly thought about the nails in his tire from the day before and wondered if whoever was responsible for that may have had something to do with this.

Looking back, I suppose Trey was right about the nails and the neighbors. Similar events started happening often—broken taillights and shattered windshields with no real explanation. Our mailbox was once torn to pieces as if someone had placed a small bomb inside of it. Every so often, we would even discover dead animals lying on our porch. Dakota was convinced a wild animal was responsible for the destruction and made a point to purchase a small handgun in case we were to catch a bear or something in the act. We all went along with his theory, but I believed deep down each of us knew it wasn't an animal doing these things.

One morning while Heather and I were heading to class, we discovered a dead crow on the front porch. I gently kicked it over with my foot to examine it and discovered the bird did not have one puncture wound on its body. It was as if something had sucked the life right out of it, leaving it stiff and completely centered on our welcome mat. Most animals leave marks on their prey—even a small house cat would have punctured the crow's flesh. Surely something powerful enough to shatter car windshields and mailboxes would have physically destroyed a small crow. It started to feel as if someone didn't want us there. My list of suspects was pretty small since there was only one house within a five-mile radius. Unfortunately, there was very little I could legally do without any proof, so I became eager to catch one of the neighbors in the act.

Trey's bedroom and mine had one window that overlooked the majority of our driveway. I purchased a spotlight that would only cut on if it sensed movement and set it so it was facing our driveway. I started keeping the window blinds raised at night so that I would notice if the spotlight turned on. I was a night owl, often staying awake studying until four in the morning. If something, or someone, were to vandalize one of our vehicles again, there was no way I'd miss it.

I didn't catch anybody being destructive toward our property, but I did begin noticing something else that was strange. Every morning, at three on the dot, I saw what appeared to be headlights shining through the trees glaring toward our house. They came from the foot of the driveway, almost like someone was about to pull in, but instead just sat there for a moment. The headlights would shine for exactly one minute and then fade out. The first few times it happened, I thought very little of it, but after multiple nights it started to spark my curiosity. I brought it to Trey's attention, only for him to insist that Roberson might be going to work and maybe I was seeing him back out of his driveway or using ours to turn around. This was a logical theory that made sense. Perhaps Roberson was an early morning worker — he had said we woke him up during the altercation over Dakota's tire.

After we had our first house party, things started to get even weirder. Whenever we had a get-together, Heather and I pretended like we didn't live in the house and were merely guests at Dakota and Trey's. This was to avoid anyone turning us in to Lincoln and causing us to face academic suspension. Dakota invited the entire football team, which meant plenty of girls would attend. Trey's little geek squad from his I.T. class was invited, and of course, Heather and I invited a few girls from our psychology class. Trey and Dakota went half and half on three kegs of beer, while Heather and I made an ABC store run to obtain everything we needed to make strawberry daiquiris.

No party was complete without a huge bonfire, so the boys made one in the front yard. Dakota had a loudspeaker system in the back of his truck, so we backed that up close to the fire and used it to supply the music. I sipped on my mixed drink as I watched people dance around the fire, and a few people make out in the yard. One girl became sick and threw up on a member of the football team, which made for good entertainment. Dakota, who desperately needed to be cut off from alcoholic beverages, started to believe he was a rapper in his drunken stupor. I managed to record a few videos of him attempting to freestyle, but all of them turned out poor due to my loud laughter. Trey, of course, was fixing someone's car stereo instead of enjoying the party like everyone else. He ate, slept, and breathed technology.

By one-o-clock in the morning, Dakota was so intoxicated Trey and Heather had to carry him to bed. He wasn't the only one. There were at least five people passed out in the yard around the bonfire, which meant it was a successful party.

The next morning I was the first one to wake up and was slightly hungover. I had a cup of coffee and a quick shower and then went to work cleaning up a little from the night before. The yard was full of red Solo cups. I grabbed a large trash bag and had begun to pick trash up when I saw what appeared to be red paint on the side of the house. I put the trash bag down and walked toward the house to gain a better look. What I saw was graffiti that read, Shhh! Don't speak! And don't look! It was written in giant letters that covered a large proportion of the vinyl siding. I took my index finger and gently ran it across the red paint, only to discover it came right off with little effort, almost like it had not begun to dry yet. I didn't want to give it a chance to dry, so I rushed inside and woke everyone up to come to help me scrub it off quickly.

Dakota was the first one up to inspect the situation. Once he saw it, he appeared confused as he mumbled the words to himself.

He stared at the graffiti with shuttered eyes. "Why would someone write this?"

"I'm not sure, but I really don't want it to stain the side of the house, so let's get it off before it dries, please," I responded. I tossed him a wet cloth.

He stepped back with his gaze still fixated on the graffiti like he was attempting to discover some hidden meaning behind the message.

"It's not dry yet?" He asked.

"No," I replied. I started scrubbing away at the graffiti. We didn't have time to procrastinate—the paint needed to be removed before it left a permanent mark on the house we were renting.

"Then, someone just did this!" He exclaimed. He stomped around, looking to see if anyone was still there.

I continued scrubbing the house. "I have been awake for the past two hours cleaning. No one is here," I assured him.

A loud screech filled the air when the front door opened and shut. Shortly after, Heather and Trey came walking around the corner toward Dakota and me.

"What's going on?" Heather asked. She turned to stare at the side of the house.

"Someone vandalized the house," Dakota answered.

Trey stepped around to take a look at the destruction. "Don't speak and don't look," he read out loud. "What does that mean?"

I started to feel annoyed with the fact that they were asking so many questions instead of helping me scrub it off. "I don't know, Trey! Can you guys please just grab a rag and help me get it off?"

"We are going to need a ladder to reach the top," Trey replied in a calm manner. He disappeared around the backside of the house where we kept the ladder.

Heather stepped closer to the graffiti and stared at it with a squint in her eyes. She gently rubbed her index finger across the paint and started studying the residue. "This isn't paint," she declared. "It's blood."

I immediately dropped my rag and looked at her with wide eyes. "Blood?"

"Yes. Blood," she responded. She leaned in to examine it closer.

A blank look came over Dakota's face. "Maybe it's just animal blood."

"Does that make it any less weird?" Heather asked in a

sarcastic yet irritated tone.

"Should we call the police?" I asked

"And tell them what, Leah? We had a party last night and woke up to find blood on the side of our house?" Dakota responded.

"He is right," Trey chimed in as he returned carrying the ladder. "If Lincoln found out we had a party last night, we would lose our scholarships. Plus, we don't know if it really is blood or not—"

"Yeah," Dakota interrupted. "I'm sure someone was just drunk and messing around last night."

The following afternoon I was prepared to go to work, only to discover a note laying in the driver's seat of my car that read, Shhh! Don't speak! I was a little taken aback by my discovery. Who would do this? And why?

I wasn't the only one that received such a note. Heather found the same message in her driver's seat. Dakota and Trey both received ones that said, Don't look. Even stranger, the spotlight had never cut on the night before to inform me that someone was outside near our vehicles.

As days passed, we started to receive notes that read, Shhh! Don't speak! And don't look, practically everywhere. They would appear in the mailbox, stuck to our front door, and even in our vehicles. We had all had enough when we finally discovered one glued to our living room plasma television. Upon peeling it off of the television screen, a sticky film was left behind. It was one thing to harass us by leaving strange notes in our vehicles, but to actually come into our house uninvited just to leave a weird note on our television was taking it too far.

Dakota became enraged. He insisted that he was going to the neighbor's house to put a stop to it. Trey, being more level headed, convinced Dakota to let him go over and talk to them first. I certainly wasn't going to allow Trey to go over there by himself, so I went with him.

Of course, they were sitting in their usual spots on the front porch, wearing the same clothing as always when we arrived. In an attempt to keep the peace, Trey didn't step a foot in the yard. Instead, he stood on the roadside and asked, "Can I talk to you guys for a minute?"

Nobody responded. They each just sat there in silence, staring at him except the young man, who held his eyes shut.

"Someone has been leaving notes for us in our vehicles and in our home. Do you guys know anything about that?" They all remained silent. "Look," Trey added. "We can take a joke, but when you start coming into our home and trespassing, that's taking it a little too far. Do you guys understand?"

At this point, I became angry when nobody responded to Trey, so I yelled, "He is talking to you! Why aren't any of you acknowledging him?" I kept in mind that a small child was sitting there listening to us, so I tried to monitor what I was saying. The young man kept his eyes shut, and the three females continued to stare blankly at me. "Is Roberson home?" I then asked.

Trey looked at me and shrugged. It didn't seem like we'd get very far with them until I remembered how to get a reaction from the young man. I walked closer and planted my feet in their yard.

Trey whispered to me, "Leah! What are you doing?"

But before I could answer, the young man stood up and started yelling, "Don't speak! Don't speak!"

My frustration spiraled. "Open your eyes!" I exclaimed out of a mixture of anger and impulse.

"I can't look!" He promptly declared back.

Something about his mannerisms sent shivers down my spine.

Roberson soon swung the front door open and stepped out on the porch. He shook his fist at the young man, causing him to flinch. "You just love waking me up, don't you!" He shouted. He then glared toward us with a wrinkled brow. "What the hell do you kids want this time?" He jerked the door behind him, causing it to slam shut.

"We just need to ask you something," Trey responded in a gentle nature.

"Well, make it quick, boy," Roberson demanded as he stood on the porch with his arms crossed.

"Have you guys been leaving notes on our property?" Trey nervously asked.

"Notes? What the hell do you mean?" Roberson asked in an aggressive manner. He tapped his boot against the porch to suggest he was growing impatient.

"Someone has been leaving notes on our property every day," Trey explained, "You guys are the only people nearby, so it has to be one of you."

Roberson unfolded his arms. With puckered lips and squinted eyes, he stepped down from the porch and came striding toward us. "Are you accusing me of writing you love

27

letters?" He asked sarcastically.

I was sick of his smart comments by that point. "They aren't love letters. They're stupid little notes, and we are getting sick of you guys coming onto our property and touching things that don't belong to you! So I'm not asking you — I'm telling you to stay the hell away from our home and keep your hands off our vehicles."

Roberson appeared shocked. Judging by his mannerisms, I wasn't sure if he had received my message or if he wanted to strangle me. "Well, look here," he replied in a hazardous voice. "A woman that doesn't know her place. You only need to speak when spoken to, okay, little lady?"

That comment was enough to spark the anger inside of Trey. "She will speak any damn time she pleases!" Trey exclaimed. "If we get one more note, I will call the police on you. Understand that?"

Roberson didn't take kindly to Trey's response. I could nearly see the steam rolling out his ears as his lips went thin, and his nostrils flared. "You are the one standing on my property right now, aren't you?" The veins bulging from his neck looked like they were going to burst at any second. "My advice to you, boy, is to go home and train your bitch how to behave like a lady and never step foot on my property again. Understand that?"

"Have you always been this ignorant?" Trey snapped back. "Is that why these ladies sitting on this porch don't speak? Have you caused them to be afraid to use their voices?"

Roberson laughed like a deranged man. "I am a real man, boy! I keep everything that crosses my path in line, including you, if you aren't careful."

At that point, Trey realized it was useless to continue arguing with someone like Roberson. Anything either of us attempted to communicate with him resolved nothing and just led to a hateful or rude response.

Trey grabbed my hand as he turned to walk away. "Just stay off of our property and stop harassing us," he demanded.

During our walk back to the house, I asked Trey what he believed the young man meant when he'd yelled, "I can't look."

"Who knows?" Trey answered. "They are all crazy as hell."

"Do you think maybe it's that guy leaving the notes? I mean, he did say he couldn't look, and the notes have been telling us not to look."

"I don't really care which one is doing it," Trey stated out of anger. "As long as they stop."

"What if he is trying to warn us or something?" I asked.

"Warn us of what?"

"I don't know—he just seems scared of Roberson. And we didn't start getting those notes until after we had the party. Maybe he is trying to tell us Roberson doesn't like a lot of noise and gets angry over it or something."

"Leah, I couldn't care less what Roberson likes. They have no business coming into our house like that. Besides, that guy never opens his eyes long enough to write a note. And even if he did, you hear how he yells at us. Doesn't sound like he would care enough to warn us about anything."

"Maybe we should just move," I suggested.

"And give that jackass exactly what he wants? No way. We need to stand our ground and show them that they aren't going to run us off like they want to."

That afternoon, things went back to normal. Trey went to work, and Dakota went to football practice. Heather and I stayed in and prepared for an exam we had the following morning. During our study session, it became clear she was growing worried over the neighbors. Any time I would ask her an academics related question, she would respond with something about the neighbors.

I finally assured her that Trey had handled it. "He made it very clear that we are not going to tolerate it any longer, and I could tell they got his message loud and clear. We will start locking the doors at night and when we are gone. And remember, Dakota has a gun if we need it." I could tell this made her feel much safer because she began to focus more on our study session.

The following morning, as Heather and I made our way to the car, I was curious to see if Trey's tactic had worked. I opened my car door, and to my surprise, there was a note sitting on the driver's seat. This time the note read, I told you not to speak! I didn't want to create any panic since Heather really needed to focus and do well on this exam. Her grades had been slipping drastically, and I knew if she saw the note, she would spend all morning thinking about it. I quickly slipped it into my back pocket and asked her if she was ready.

"Yeah, I guess so," she announced and buckled her seat belt. "No note today?"

"Nope," I responded. "Looks like Trey ended that."

A look of relief immediately came over her face. "Thank God!" she said. She glanced down at her fingernails. "Now, I just need to pass this exam and get my nails retouched."

After taking the exam, I had planned to tell Heather about the note, but the more I thought about it, the more I was convinced it wasn't the best choice. She aced her exam, which was a cause for celebration. I didn't want the ongoing drama with the neighbors to rain on her parade. Not to mention the fact that I didn't want Trey or Dakota confronting Roberson anymore. Both of them, especially Dakota, seemed ready to fight over the harassment we were receiving, and I honestly wasn't sure what Roberson was capable of. As devoted as I was to understanding complex human behavior, even I found him to be unpredictable. Trey and Dakota were strong, but even together, I didn't believe they would have stood a fair chance against someone the size of Roberson.

With all of this in mind, I thought it would be best if I just kept the note to myself. I honestly didn't believe we were in any danger. Instead, my instinct told me the neighbors were probably just harassing us because we were too loud during the party we'd thrown. I assumed they were using childish tactics to force us to move away. My goal was to simply ignore them. It was clear that they wanted some sort of reaction from us. They wanted to know their tactics bothered us. Maybe if we stopped giving them exactly what they wanted by confronting them and making a scene, they would grow tired of their pointless harassment strategies and stop. My only hope was that Dakota did not receive a note. I could convince Trey to let it go, but I knew I would have a hard time talking Dakota out of another one of his anger spells. Thankfully, when Heather called Dakota to inform him of how well she did on her exam, he didn't mention a note. Instead, he sounded overjoyed for her, which convinced me that he must not have received anything in his vehicle that morning.

That night we decided to rent a few movies and order pizza to celebrate Heather's hard work. She definitely deserved it since she'd finally put effort into something other than shopping. Trey and Dakota picked up a few RedBox movies, along with three large pepperoni pizzas, on their way home. It soon became clear to Heather and me that we should've picked out the movies. The guys came home with the complete Jurassic Park series and Godzilla, which was not something Heather and I were set on watching.

As Jurassic Park began to play, we gossiped about school. I listened to Heather, Dakota, and Trey share laughs about a fellow student that apparently peed his pants in class a few days ago, and I gained a sense of peace. I thought about the fact that all four of us wanted this home so that we could have freedom and share experiences like this together. Nights like this particular one were exactly why we'd left campus and what we all dreamed of having. There was no way I was going to allow the neighbors to take that from us.

As midnight approached, and we ran out of pizza, Dakota looked at Trey and said, "Thanks, man."

"For what, buddy?" Trey asked, still chewing his final bite of pizza.

"For handling the dumbasses across the street. I didn't

get any corny letters today, so I think they got the message."

"Oh, no problem. I'm just glad they got the hint," Trey responded. "Make sure you guys lock your car doors, just in case."

Dakota started walking toward the bathroom. "I checked everyone's doors. They are all locked."

I knew Trey too well and could tell by his lack of enthusiasm he wasn't mentioning something. Later that night, when we were getting ready for bed, I asked him if he got a note. He hesitated for a moment. "Yeah. Just the same stupid thing."

I gave my pillow a few jabs to fluff it. "What did yours say?" I asked.

"I told you not to look, or something lame like that."

"I got one too," I announced.

"I figured. When I noticed mine, I assumed they left one for you as well due to our alteration yesterday. Let me guess — yours said something like, 'I told you not to speak'?" He laughed to make lite of the situation.

"Yup!" I exclaimed, "They want a reaction from us."

"Well, we aren't going to give them one anymore."

I agreed with him. "They are trying to play cat and mouse games. The best thing we can do is just ignore them."

"I just don't want them inside of our home or vehicles," he said. "Everything is locked up now, and my car has a sensitive alarm system, so good luck getting inside."

I truly believed ignoring the neighbors would work, but little did I know they were just getting started.

I laid in bed studying the following night while Trey slept beside me, as usual. As 3 a.m. approached, I glanced up from my notes and focused my attention toward the window when something startled me. As the headlights cut on and gleamed through the trees surrounding our front yard like they did every night, the glare outlined a dark figure. The figure stood in our yard approximately fifteen yards from the window, and it appeared to be the outline of a human. It was such a dark, cloudy night that I was unable to make out any details, like facial features or clothing. I could only tell something, or someone was standing in our yard. Without hesitation, I shook Trey to inform him that someone was outside. As soon as he awoke and rolled over to see what was going on, the headlights cut off.

He turned to me with half closed eyes. "What's wrong?"

"Someone is outside!" I panicked.

Trey quickly jumped out of bed and bolted toward the front door, determined to catch whoever it was red handed. Worried about his safety, I ran after him. When I stepped out onto the front porch, I saw Trey walking around the yard using his cellphone as a flashlight.

"I don't see anything."

"Someone was out here—I saw them," I stated.

He shined his phone around, studying the yard. "Where did you see them?"

"Right over there," I responded, pointing toward the area where I'd seen the figure.

As Trey approached the area, the spotlight cut on, revealing nobody but Trey standing there. "Are you sure it was a person and not a tree or something?" He asked as the front door swung open and Heather came out in her nightgown.

"What's going on, you guys?" She asked as if she had been awakened by our commotion. Her eyes were half shut, and she let out a big yawn as she stood there awaiting an explanation.

"Nothing. I thought I saw something, but I guess it was just a tree," I replied.

"It's after three in the morning. You guys need to get some sleep." She turned around and went back inside.

We returned to bed after Trey assured me I probably just saw a tree or something. Even though I verbally agreed with him, I knew it wasn't a tree. I saw those headlights every night, but never had I seen a tree shaped like a human standing in the yard. Before returning to bed, I glanced out the window once more. The spotlight was still activated from Trey walking through its range. I could see clearly that whatever I had just seen was no longer standing there. Why had the spotlight cut on when it sensed Trey walking through the area, but not for the strange figure?

The next morning Dakota's yelling and cursing woke everyone in the house. As Trey and I met Heather in the living room to see what was going on, we noticed the front door was wide open. We all made our way outside onto the front porch, where Dakota was standing next to four dead rabbits. "Look at this shit!" He exclaimed. "I bet the neighbors did this!"

"Dakota! Calm down!" Trey demanded.

Heather turned to go back inside. "It's too early for this."

Dakota finally denounced his belief that wild animals were killing and leaving the animals on our porch, which I'd always known wasn't the case. While Trey attempted to calm Dakota, I kneeled down to examine the bunnies closer. Using the broom on the front porch, propped up against the house, I flipped the rabbits over, only to notice they had no marks on them. Surely something was killing all of the animals being left on our porch, but what? Were they poisoned?

Just when I was about to go inside to retrieve a trash bag to dispose of them, an idea hit me. I had been checking the animals externally, searching for a sign of death, only to discover they had no visible wounds. However, I had not examined any of the animals internally. Perhaps by taking a look in the mouths of these rabbits, I would discover something.

"Hey," I announced to interrupt Trey and Dakota's dispute. "One of you grab me something to pry their mouths open."

Both of them looked at me in disgust.

"What?" Trey asked in a confused tone.

"Eew!" Dakota exclaimed with a crinkled nose. "Why?"

"Just do it!" I demanded.

Dakota, who still looked disturbed by my request, reached in his pocket and tossed me his pocketknife. I pried the first rabbit's mouth open and noticed a lot of blood surrounding its teeth and gums. Upon closer inspection, I discovered its tongue was missing.

"Look at this, guys. The tongue is gone."

"What?" Dakota asked out of complete confusion. "Why would someone cut a rabbit's tongue out?" He walked up behind me to get a glimpse of the rabbit's mouth. He was completely grossed out when he saw the carnage and immediately turned around and covered his mouth.

"I'm not sure," I answered as I continued to inspect the rabbits.

Trey bent down to help me examine them. "This one has a tongue," he informed me.

After pausing to think for a moment, I pulled the bunny's eyelid open to expose that its eyes were missing. After examining all four rabbits, we discovered two were missing tongues, and two were missing their eyes. We were confused, to say the least, as we sat there in silence, trying to figure out why someone would do this.

Trey eventually broke the silence. "The notes. The notes say, don't speak and don't look." He looked at me. "And the rabbits are missing their tongues and eyes."

"So what?" Dakota asked. "They are using dead animals to tell us not to speak and look?"

Trey looked at me with a serious expression and said, "Hand me your car keys."

I could tell he was on a mission, so without hesitating, I went inside and retrieved them from my purse and tossed them to him.

"You're not going over to their house, are you?" I asked.

He rushed down the steps and marched toward the driveway. "No," he replied. "I'm checking the vehicles."

I walked over to assist him. He unlocked my car door and scavenged through the front seat. To my surprise, he pulled out a note and held it up for me to see.

"How did they open my door?" I asked out of utter

confusion.

"I don't know," Trey responded.

Dakota bolted toward his truck. "That's impossible! There's no way anyone could open my truck without the key." He unlocked his vehicle, only to discover a note glued to his steering wheel. Dakota crumbled the note up and tossed it onto the ground, then circled his truck, closely inspecting it for any damage.

"You guys don't suppose one of them broke into the house last night and took our keys, do you?" I panicked.

Dakota and Trey both looked at each other, suggesting they were considering the thought I had planted, when Trey finally realized, "The front and back doors were both locked."

"They broke in somehow!" Dakota declared.

I pressed my face against the driver's side window on Heather's locked vehicle and saw a folded piece of paper sitting in her driver's seat. "Heather got one too."

Trey walked over to his own car and pulled on the door handle, which forced his obnoxious alarm system to sound off. He immediately shut it off, unlocked it, and removed a note that was glued to his seat. "You guys tell me how anyone could've tampered with my car without forcing the alarm to go off," he asked in a way that suggested he didn't really expect an answer.

In full-blown rage, Dakota returned to the porch, where he picked one of the rabbits up by its hind legs and stormed off down the driveway toward the neighbors' house. I yelled for him to stop.

"No! I'm done with their bullshit!" He yelled back as he

continued making his way down the driveway.

"Maybe we should just call the police," I suggested.

After pausing for a moment to suggest that he was considering my suggestion, Dakota turned around and made his way back up the driveway. "I have to get ready for practice anyways. Just call the police and let them deal with it." He dropped the rabbit onto the ground and stormed inside.

I could sense Dakota was a little afraid but didn't want to admit it. It just wasn't in his nature to let go of his tough guy persona and make himself appear vulnerable. I pulled out my cell phone and dialed 911.

CHAPTER 3
WHERE IS OFFICER TAYLOR?

Trey and I gathered on the front porch as we waited for the police to arrive. I may have gotten a total of three hours of sleep the night before, and though my body was exhausted, my mind was wide-awake. I stood there in silence, wondering why anyone would want to harm animals like the rabbits on our porch. What could a small defenseless animal have possibly done to deserve such trauma? As a child, my father had hunted and kept plenty of fresh meat on the table. I was taught that you do not kill anything that isn't causing any harm unless you plan to eat it. It was almost sacrilegious for me to see an animal that had been tortured in such a way, only to be left in the spring heat to rot. Removing the tongue and eyes from a rabbit served no purpose other than being a scare tactic of some sort. What were the neighbors trying to tell us? And why were they using such harsh remedies to spread their message? We knew we were not welcomed as far as they were concerned, but for the most part, we didn't bother them. Why did they want to frighten us so badly?

Trey and I glanced at the driveway when the sound of gravel crunching echoed through the air. Through the trees, I could see what appeared to be an SUV with police lights on top heading up the driveway. Once the police car parked, Trey and I greeted the officer as he stepped out of his car while Heather slept, and Dakota got ready for football practice.

The officer strolled toward us with his hat tilted low, hiding his eyes. "Good morning, I'm Officer Taylor." He pushed his hat upward above his brow and stood stiff. "I received a call about a disturbance. Want to tell me what seems to be going on?"

Officer Taylor immediately looked down after his introduction, focusing his attention on the dead rabbits lying on the porch. He snarled his nose in a manner of disgust and took a small step back.

Trey explained how we'd discovered the rabbits lying there stiff and lifeless shortly before we called. I interrupted to inform the officer that this wasn't the first time we'd awakened to find dead animals lying perfectly centered on our welcome mat.

"I was informed that you guys are also receiving strange letters?" He asked.

I nodded my head and handed him one of the notes we discovered before his arrival.

"We get them pretty much every day. They have left them in our mailbox, vehicles, and have even come into our home, sticking them to our television," I declared.

"And you say it's the neighbors doing this?" Officer Taylor asked.

41

"Yes, sir," Trey answered, rubbing the back of his neck.

"Well, I'm going to go on down here and have a little chat with your neighbors real quick. If you guys can just hang tight for a little while," Officer Taylor stated.

We watched as Officer Taylor drove down the driveway toward the neighbor's house. I was eager for him to put a stop to the harassment we had been receiving and couldn't wait for him to return and tell us what they had to say for themselves. I wanted them arrested for trespassing and hoped he would be very harsh on them for what they had done.

He wasn't gone any longer than ten minutes before he came back up the driveway. As he stepped out of his vehicle, I had a ton of questions. "What happened? Did they speak to you?"

"Doesn't appear to be anyone home."

I glared over at Trey in a state of confusion. "What? That's impossible. They are always home sitting on their front porch. Sir, they literally never move from that porch."

"Well, no one's there right now, I assure you of that. I even took a look through the windows, and it doesn't look like anyone has been home for a long time."

"What do you mean?" Trey asked with a lost expression on his face.

"It was just a lot of dust and cobwebs all of the place. Are you guys sure people live there?" Officer Taylor asked, appearing just as confused as we were.

We assured him that people definitely occupied the home and explained to him that they appeared to be very dirty people. I honestly wasn't surprised to hear they lived that way.

"I tell you what," Officer Taylor began. "I do not believe you guys are in any real danger here. Sounds like someone is just trying to pick at you all. What I'll do is ride through later on, and when I see them outside, I'll have a chat with them. How does that sound?"

Trey glanced at me and shrugged his shoulders to suggest there was nothing more we could really do at the moment. "I guess that will have to work."

"Just be sure to keep your stuff locked up, and I'll handle it as soon as I can. You kids have a good day," Officer Taylor concluded.

As he drove away. I mumbled sarcastically, "Thanks for all of your help." Then added, "What a waste of time!"

Trey, who shared my disbelief that the neighbors weren't home, hopped in his car and started the engine.

"Where are you going?" I asked.

"I'll be right back," he said. He took off down the driveway.

I stood in the driveway with my arms crossed, waiting for him to return. I suspected he was checking for himself to see if the neighbors were home since neither of us could really believe they weren't. No more than two minutes later, he returned. As he parked his car and shut the engine off, I asked him what he was doing. He told me that the neighbors were all there sitting on their front porch, just like always. We assumed they must have seen the police coming to our house and hid.

"Should we call 911 again?" I asked.

"No," Trey stated. He stepped out of his vehicle and shut the door. "He said he would drive through later. He will get them."

We went about our day as we normally would. Trey went to work, Dakota left for practice, and Heather and I headed to class. On our way, Heather randomly asked, "Why do you think that guy keeps his eyes closed?" I shrugged and shook my head, suggesting I had no idea. "You think he's blind or something?"

"I suppose he could be," I replied.

"Maybe they are mentally challenged," she suggested. "That could be why they don't speak and just stare at us."

"Even mentally challenged people speak. And you would think the little girl would play once in a while, or at least attend school." It was definitely odd to see anyone, especially a child, always sitting on a front porch in the exact same spot, even during school hours. Most children that age had a ton of energy and always ran around finding something to get into, but not this one.

"Could be homeschooled," Heather announced.

"They don't really strike me as the type of people that are suited to teach a child." I chuckled to myself as I envisioned one of the mutes attempting to teach someone English or math.

"Do you think they hid from the police?" Heather asked.

"Had to," I declared. "He actually walked onto the porch and looked through their window, and said he didn't see anyone."

"They must have enough sense to know they could get in

a lot of trouble," Heather added.

I nodded my head to agree with her statement.

The subject was eventually changed when Heather's favorite song came on the radio. She cranked the volume up and started singing along while dancing in the passenger seat. I admired her free spirited and carefree nature. I had often longed to be more like that and to break the chains of responsibility that held me down. I was always worried about my grades, bills, and preparing for the future. Heather just seemed so content living in the present, and it seemed to me that was the way life was meant to be lived.

After class that afternoon we went shopping. It felt good to actually go out and enjoy my life for a moment instead of coming straight home to prepare for the following day. It wasn't something I often did because Heather was known to literally force people to shop until they dropped, but when I did, I usually had a great time with her.

We returned home after our shopping adventure around 9 p.m. and were greeted by three police cars in our driveway. Flashing blue and red lights filled the yard, and a good portion of the porch. Thoughts immediately flooded my mind. What was going on? Had something happened with the neighbors while we were gone? Perhaps Officer Taylor stayed true to his word and found them sitting outside. Heather made her concern well known as we headed up the driveway—it was safe to say she was as worried as I was.

As we pulled in, I noticed Trey standing on the porch talking to three police officers, including one who appeared to be writing down something on a note pad. The other two officers were practically breaking their necks to stare at Heather and me as we parked the vehicle. Eager to discover what was going on, Heather and I rushed to unbuckle our seatbelts and step out.

As we walked heavily toward the porch, I could hear one of the officers talking. "And you didn't see him anymore?"

Trey appeared calm and collected, which gave me a slight sense of relief.

"Is everything okay?" I asked. Heather stood beside me with her arms crossed, curious to hear a response to my question.

"Yes, ma'am," one of the officers responded. "I believe this young man has answered all of our questions."

I glanced over at Trey, making eye contact with him. "The officer from this morning, Officer Taylor, never reported back to work. They haven't heard from him since."

My heart sank to my stomach. "What?!" I exclaimed. "You guys don't know where he is?"

"No," an officer answered. "We talked to him on his two-way radio shortly after he left here. Haven't heard from him since."

"Maybe he just went home or something," Heather suggested, still standing by me with her arms folded.

"His shift ended hours ago, but he never came into the station to clock out. We stopped by his house, and he isn't there," one of the officers said to us.

The officer that had been writing things down put his notepad away. "I'm sure he will turn up. He is a pretty impulsive guy, so it's hard to say where he is. I appreciate your cooperation and answering our questions. If you kids see anything, give me a call." The officer preceded to hand Trey his business card.

"I definitely will," Trey stated. "I hope he turns up real soon."

While Trey looked at the business card the officer handed him, Heather and I watched them as they drove down the driveway. Questions raced through my mind. Where was Officer Taylor? Was he okay? Would he return? Why didn't he report back to the station at the end of his shift? It just didn't feel right. I could tell Heather was lost in thought as well. She stood beside me, completely zoned out.

"What do you guys think happened to him?"

"Oh, I'm sure he's fine. He's a police officer—maybe he just went to inspect something and got caught up and lost track of time." Trey added, "He will turn up."

I sat up and watched television with Heather until Dakota came home later that night. Afterward, I announced I was heading off to bed, where Trey lay sound asleep. I raised the window blinds, which was part of my nightly routine by that time. This particular night I was exhausted and barely able to hold my eyes open. Determined to stay awake until 3 a.m., I sat up in the bed with my legs crossed and tried focusing on homework. I was eager to pay close attention when the headlights cut on and gleamed through the trees toward our home. I wanted to determine if it really was a tree, or something else, that I had seen the night before. I made sure every light was off in the room to prevent any glares from inside, distorting my view through the glass window.

At 2:59, I turned my attention toward the window and waited. As the minute passed, the headlights turned on, revealing the figure standing there once again. This time I had no doubt that it was definitely a person. It looked as if they were facing the window, watching me as I watched them. My first reaction was to shake Trey and inform him someone was out there. Then it hit me—by the time he was fully awake, the headlights would turn off, and the figure would be gone, just as it had happened the night before. I knew I had approximately forty seconds left until the headlights cut off, so instead of waking Trey up, I decided to quickly run out onto the porch myself.

As I placed my hand on the doorknob to walk outside and confront the individual, fear completely overtook me. I had no idea who was standing in the yard or what might happen once I stepped out that door. I hesitated for a split second, took a deep breath, and opened the front door.

After stepping out onto the porch, I saw the dark figure standing in the yard. "Can I help you with something?" I shouted. At first, the figure just stood there and remained silent, so I spoke up again, "Roberson? Is that you? You realize you are trespassing, right? We have spoken to the police." At that point, the figure appeared to move its head in my direction to suggest that, whoever it was, they were listening to me.

All of a sudden, a bone-chilling whisper filled the air, causing goosebumps to emerge over my flesh. "Shh...don't speak."

A breeze gushed across my face as the headlights cut off,

leaving me standing there on the porch in complete darkness. My heart thumped, and I turned to run toward the door. To my dismay, the door wouldn't open, as if someone had locked it behind me.

The haunting whisper pierced the air again. "Shh... don't speak." But this time, it sounded much closer than it had before. I screamed at the top of my lungs and beat on this door, hoping someone would hear my cries and come to my rescue. The eerie whisper crept closer and closer until it sounded like someone was making their way onto the porch where I was standing. "Shh...don't speak."

I screamed as loud as I possibly could and banged on the door with every ounce of strength I had in me. Finally, right beside me, as if someone were whispering directly into my ear, I heard, "Shh...don't speak," accompanied by a cold breath beating against my cheek as the voice spoke to me.

At that exact moment, the porch light flicked on, revealing nobody standing there with me. Dakota swung the door open, and all I could do was grab onto him and cry.

"What's wrong, Leah? Are you okay?" He hugged me with force.

"There was someone out here!" I exclaimed with tears running down my face. "The door was jammed, and I couldn't get inside."

"Someone was out here?" He asked as he removed his hands from around me and walked out onto the porch. He paced around frantically, looking for someone. "I don't see anyone."

"They were out here, I swear!"

"Go bring me the gun in my nightstand," he demanded without taking his eyes off the porch.

After taking him the gun and a flashlight, he instructed me to return inside and stay there. About fifteen minutes later, he came marching inside and told me that nobody was out there. "I must have scared whoever it was off. Don't go out there by yourself like that anymore, Leah."

I wiped the tears from my face and cleared my throat. "This isn't the first time I've seen someone out there, Dakota." He glared at me as if he was waiting for me to explain what I meant by my statement. "Someone was out there last night too. And every night, at exactly three in the morning, headlights shine toward our house."

He took a seat next to me on the sofa. "Headlights? Like a car?"

"Yeah. Every night they cut on and beam up the driveway and into our yard for exactly one minute."

"The neighbors are doing this?" He asked in a concerned tone.

"I guess, yeah. The lights come from the direction of their house. Trey and I thought maybe Roberson just went to work at three. I figured I was just seeing his headlights as he pulled out of his driveway." I paused for a moment. "I don't think that's what it is, though, Dakota."

He appeared to be lost in thought, gazing at me with still eyes. "You think he's purposely shining his lights up here? Maybe trying to see us or something?"

"Maybe. I don't really know," I responded. "I just think it's weird that it happens at three on the dot every night."

I went on to explain the creepy whispers I had heard outside as Dakota listened compassionately. I was surprised when he didn't become angry and storm outside prepared to fight.

"Well, tonight, we will all stay up until three, okay? We will catch the assholes. If I see any of them standing in this yard, I promise I'll take care of them once and for all."

CHAPTER 4
THERE'S A MONSTER WITH YOU

I woke up around two the following afternoon. It was Friday, and school was officially closed for spring break. The last time I'd slept so late was during my high school years, but my body desperately needed the rest. As soon as I opened my eyes and started to stretch, the smell of food cooking entered my nose. I couldn't quite make out what the smell was — bacon? Or maybe it was steak? Whatever it was, it smelt amazing.

I tied my hair in a bun and made my way into the kitchen, where Trey stood over the stove cooking hamburgers. "Good afternoon, sleepyhead," he announced. He looked at me from the corner of his eye, grinning.

Immediately I heard laughter coming from the living room. I looked over to discover Dakota and Heather watching some sort of standup comedienne on television. Dakota's laughter concluded when he focused his attention toward me. "How are you feeling today?"

"I heard about last night. Girl, that is freaking insane,"

Heather stated.

"I'm okay," I replied, still trying to fully wake up.

"I'm making lunch," Trey announced. "Or in your case, breakfast."

"Shut up!" I replied sarcastically, nudging him in the arm.

"I'm kidding. You needed to sleep in."

I took my seat on the sofa next to Heather. Trey asked each of us what we wanted on our hamburgers. We each shouted out our orders.

"Come and get it," Trey announced, causing Dakota and Heather to jump up and rush into the kitchen.

Trey hand-delivered mine. He stole Heather's spot on the sofa and sat down next to me. "You okay?" He bit down into his burger and quickly discovered it was still too hot to eat. He started to breathe deeply in and out of his mouth in an attempt to cool the food sitting on his tongue.

I giggled at his stupidity. "Yeah, I'm good."

"Dakota told me what happened. Why didn't you wake me up?"

I shrugged. "By the time you would've gotten up, it would've been too late."

"Who do you think it was?" Heather asked as she came carrying her plate into the living room.

"I'm not really sure. Probably one of the jerks across the street," I answered.

"You know it was. Probably trying to stick another note in one of our cars," Trey stated.

"I have a surprise for the lucky asshole that crosses me next time," Dakota announced.

I waited for my hamburger to cool while we all sat and watched a comedy show. Trey chuckled at the television with a mouth full of food. Even though he was a far stretch away from elegance, he was still so handsome to me. His hair was sticking up in all different directions as if he woke up and never bothered to fix it. Ketchup stretched across his lower lip, but it took him a while to notice it and wipe it off. His cinnamon brown eyes always seemed to be filled with joy and innocence. It felt good to be beside him, knowing neither of us had anywhere to be. We could just sit there and actually enjoy each other for a moment. It seemed that every free second we had anymore revolved around drama. I was tired of allowing the neighbors to dictate my emotional state. We'd escaped Lincoln's insane policies, but for what? Did we really find peace? Or did we just land ourselves in another situation full of restraint? I didn't want to spend the remainder of my college years playing cat and mouse games with the neighbors.

"Let's do something tonight," Trey suggested. "Forget the neighbors and all the drama. It's Friday, damn it—let's have fun."

"I'm down!" Heather exclaimed. She jumped to her feet, impulsively. "Oh! There is a new store a few towns over, and they have—"

"We aren't going shopping, babe," Dakota interrupted, causing Heather to return to her seat disappointed.

Dakota glanced at me. "What do you think? Want to get outta here?"

I thought about it for a moment. Getting out of that house actually sounded like a perfect idea. "As long as we do something fun," I said.

Dakota grinned. "Hell yeah. I'll handle the assholes as soon as we get back, cool?" He stuck out his fist, waiting for me to gently punch it with my own.

I bumped his fist. "Cool," I replied.

The four of us started scheming up ideas of what we could do that weekend. It didn't take us long to start ignoring Heather's suggestions since they all revolved around shoe shopping. Trey proposed camping. Dakota seemed interested, but Heather refused.

"I don't do nature."

Dakota expressed how badly he wanted to go fishing, attempting to change Heather's mind.

"It's not happening," she continued, digging in her heels. "No way I'm sleeping in a tent."

"Okay, what about this?" Trey proposed. "We could stay the weekend at the lake."

"Clear Water's Lake?" Dakota's interest was piqued.

"Yeah. It's only like, what? An hour away," Trey said. "We could rent a cabin on the lake for the weekend. The girls don't have to camp, and we get to fish."

"That sounds good to me," I stated, hoping Heather would agree.

We gazed at her, waiting to hear her response.

"A lake trip would be cool," she said with a nod. "I've been wanting to check out Clear Water's anyways."

"Woo-Hoo!" Dakota shouted. "We are going to the lake, baby!" He clapped his hands together loudly and jolted up from the sofa. He informed us that he would look up the number and reserve a lakefront cabin for the weekend.

"Make sure it has cable, Wi-Fi, and A/C!" Heather insisted. Honestly, I was glad she made those requests. I looked forward to getting away for a few nights, but I definitely didn't want to be stuck on a lake with no television, Internet, or A/C. There are just some basic things a person needs if they are to enjoy a weekend getaway.

Trey and I jumped in the shower together so that we could get ready before packing up our things. Dakota and Heather ran to the store to purchase fishing poles and a few necessities we would need during the weekend.

We packed everything into Trey's car since it had the most room. Dakota, who had already started drinking, begged for me to let him have the front seat. I did not really mind riding in the back with Heather and letting the boys have the front, so I didn't argue with Dakota and let him have his way.

As we headed down the driveway to begin our journey, Dakota tore a piece of paper out of a notebook Trey had lying on his floorboard. He found a highlighter in the console and used his teeth to remove the top from it. I watched as he wrote, Screw you! in large print, nearly covering the piece of paper. I think we were all a little unsure why he was writing this, but because he was slightly intoxicated, nobody mentioned anything.

As we pulled out of the driveway, I noticed the neighbors sitting on their front porch, glaring at us, like always. The old woman gently rocked back and forth with the same green ball of yarn sitting in her lap. I was not sure what she was knitting when she wasn't busy staring at us, but it seemed to be taking her a long time to finish. The middle-aged woman, still in her usual seat across the porch from the old lady, held her baby bundled up in the same pink blanket. The little girl sat with her legs crossed, right beside the middle-aged woman. And the young man, still seated on the porch steps, held his eyes shut. Everything remained the same, day in and day out. The people never changed positions, always wore the same clothes, and never seemed to move too much. They never smiled and never grew tired of staring at us any time we were at the bottom of the driveway.

I guess I couldn't say much anymore because, at that point, I found myself always staring at them as well. Even though I always knew what clothes they would have on, where they would be sitting, and how they would be staring, I found it nearly impossible not to look over at them every chance I could. There was something so odd about them, and it just seemed to spark my curiosity. I had always found them to be creepy, but this particular afternoon I couldn't help but feel a little sorry for them. I don't know why, but there was just something about the lack of expression on their faces that put a small lump in my throat. They seemed drained of energy, almost like they were all too tired to smile or display emotion. I supposed there may have been something going on inside that caused them to feel more at home outside.

As the sadness began to take over me, Dakota interrupted my train of thought.

"Stop real quick."

Trey hit the brakes on the car, coming to a halt right in front of the neighbors' home.

"Hey!" Dakota shouted out the window toward them. "Here's a note for you, assholes!" He crumbled the piece of notebook paper up into a ball and threw it into their yard. Afterward, he held his middle finger up for them to see as Trey pulled away.

The boys shared a laugh and joked about the event. "Did you see the freak with his eyes closed?" Dakota laughed.

Even though they harassed us daily and had scared me the night before, what Dakota did just didn't sit right with me. It felt wrong. I had witnessed Roberson's poor attitude and found myself wondering if he was abusive. We couldn't possibly know the lives those people lived. The last thing I wanted to do was play their games.

"You shouldn't have done it," I declared.

Dakota turned around to glance at me. The narrowing of his eyebrows caused his forehead to wrinkle as he gave me a confused yet angry expression. "Shouldn't have done what? Thrown a damn letter in their yard?"

"I don't want to play games with them."

Trey, who was focused on driving, joined in. "Wow, Leah. After everything they've done, why are you defending them?"

"I'm not!" I quickly responded to defend myself. "I'm just saying, what does that accomplish?"

"It accomplishes giving me a good laugh," Dakota replied. He turned on the radio and scanned through stations.

"Roberson practically assaulted you last night," Trey said, speaking over top of the shuffling music, commercials, and broadcasters.

I paused for a moment. "We don't know who it was, Trey. Nobody hurt me or anything."

"So you think we should do nothing. Just sit back and take their bullshit?" Dakota asked with a hint of sarcasm.

"No. Not at all," I replied. "I'm saying we should confront them when we catch them in our yard instead of picking fights with them."

"I agree with Leah," Heather added.

Trey and Dakota shared a laugh as if something I said was funny. "Yeah, Dakota!" Trey sarcastically shouted. "Don't be mean to the poor neighbors. God knows they don't bother anyone." The two continued to laugh, but I ignored them.

We arrived at the lake around eight that evening. The cabin was much more luxurious than I imagined it would be. Upon walking in, I glanced up to appreciate the high ceilings; I had never had the pleasure of seeing anything so elegant in person. On one side of the living room were two large sliding glass doors that led to a decent sized deck, which overlooked the lake. The sun had gone down, making it hard to admire the view we would share that weekend. Regardless, the moonlight still glistened upon the water, and the faint sound of ripples filled the air as the smell of the lake water entered our nostrils. What a refreshing getaway this was already becoming.

We turned around and went back inside to make ourselves at home for the weekend. Dakota, who planned to go catfishing that night, went to work prepping his fishing pole. He ripped off the plastic that had protected the reel while it sat on a shelf in a store. Grabbing onto the end of the fishing line that was wrapped tightly around the reel, he pulled it and threaded it through each eye on the pole. As he tied a hook on the end of the line, using his teeth to strengthen the knot, the hook slightly stabbed his index finger. Blood began to flow from the tiny wound. He rushed into the kitchen, grabbing a paper towel to hold over it.

Trey teased him. "Good going, man. Real smooth."

Trey's eyes eventually caught a glimpse of a remote control sitting on a coffee table in front of the living room sofa. He picked it up and cut the television on, revealing that whoever rented the cabin last had left the television on the local news channel.

Meanwhile, Heather, who was unboxing alcoholic beverages and placing them in the refrigerator, asked, "Who else is getting lit tonight?" That was her way of searching for a drinking buddy.

Without hesitating, I walked over and removed the Red's Apple Ale she was about to place in the refrigerator from her hand. I opened it and took a few sips before I started to assist her with unboxing the beer.

Trey signaled for me to toss him one as he skimmed through the TV guide, searching for something to watch. "Get my pole ready, too," he told Dakota. "Did you get the chicken liver?"

I expressed my disgust by crinkling up my nose.

"Don't worry, it's not for us," Heather assured me. "Apparently catfish are fans of chicken liver. Yeah. We got it," she shouted to Trey.

About that time, something on television caught our

attention. I walked toward Trey, who was standing behind the sofa, still flipping through the TV guide with the news channel minimized into the corner of the TV screen.

"Exit that out," I demanded, forcing him to click cancel on the remote control, causing the TV guide to close out.

On the news was a picture of Officer Taylor. We gathered around to listen as the news anchor began to speak.

"William Taylor, a police officer in Rockwood, has been missing for more than two days. Authorities say he did not return to the station at the end of his shift Wednesday night after investigating a disturbance call he received that morning. Police are asking anyone that may have any information on Officer Taylor's whereabouts to come forward. Information at this time is limited, but an investigation to find him has begun. We at channel eleven news will keep viewers updated as we discover more details."

We stood there in utter confusion. What could have happened to Officer Taylor? Could he have wrecked his car somewhere? I could not wrap my mind around it as I stood there searching for answers.

"That's crazy." Heather returned to the kitchen to grab a beer. "I hope the poor dude is okay."

Dakota returned to the fishing poles and started prepping them to go catfishing. "Sucks. Hope he didn't wreck or something." He let out a loud burp and continued. "Hey baby, grab me a beer, please."

"I thought the same thing," I admitted. "Maybe he wrecked his car off a bank or something."

"Might have," Trey agreed.

Everyone just seemed to be making lite of the situation. It was not like we had a personal relationship with Officer Taylor—we'd only met him one time. So why did I feel so disturbed about his disappearance? Perhaps it was because I was one of the last people to see him. Whatever the reason was, it bothered me greatly to know he still had not been found. Whatever happened to him, I wanted to enjoy the weekend. Drama seemed to always follow us, ever since we left campus. We deserved one peaceful weekend without worry. Even though it sat heavily on my mind, I didn't mention another word about Officer Taylor. Instead, I went fishing with Trey, Dakota, Heather, and a cooler full of beer.

We sat on a little sandy spot along the edge of the lake that night and watched the boys fish. A man and little boy, who I assumed to be father and son, shared the little lake beach with us. They stood a few yards away from us to suggest they wanted space to themselves. Trey made a little fire for Heather and me to sit by. It was very relaxing and peaceful, to say the least.

I watched the little boy fiddle around, searching for something to entertain himself. He couldn't have been a day older than six. His laughter and the way he pranced around his father brought a smile to my face. There was just something so sweet and innocent about children that always seemed to bring a sense of peace and joy to my soul. The light from our campfire danced across his cute little face as he twiddled around his father. He wore a small fisherman's cap, a miniature version of the one his father was wearing. It was obvious he was growing restless while he waited, along with his father, for a fish to bite. He kicked at the sand with his little feet and kneeled down frequently to stick his hand into the water. A few times, he attempted to run off, forcing his father to command him to remain by his side. The two of them had a small lantern that the child used to make shadow puppets, which humored me to watch.

The child's small fishing pole, which was placed in a pole holder stuck in the sand, tilted downward. A tiny bell attached to the pole jingled, alerting the pair that something was messing with the line. "You got a bite," the man stated. He picked the child's fishing pole up and gave it a jerk. "It's on there good. Come on and reel it in." The man handed the pole over to the child.

The boy seemed to be putting forth every ounce of strength he had each time he managed to turn the reel. His lips were puckered, and he groaned. His father kneeled down next to him and said, "You got it. Keep on reeling." Once the child managed to get the fish close to the shoreline, the man took over the fishing pole and used a small net to pull it onto the sandy bank. "That's a nice catfish, son. Good job," he stated proudly.

"He was heavy," the boy said as he glanced down at the fish.

While the man worked to remove the fish from the hook, the little boy glanced over at us like he had just noticed us sitting there. His eyes grew large as if he were face to face with a ghost or something. I figured the little guy must have been uncomfortable with a group of strangers sitting near him watching his big moment. Either it was getting too late for the child to be out, or the man couldn't fit any more fish in the cooler they had because they gathered up their things to leave.

As they made their way past us, Trey attempted to make small talk, "That was a nice catch."

"Thanks," the man responded hastily as he continued walking away, carrying his baggage. The little boy lagged behind his father but stopped to stare at us once more. "Brandon, come on," the man yelled out, breaking the little boy's trance.

"Cute kid," Heather said, watching them walk toward the cabin next to ours. "You guys having any luck? Or is that kid about to school you both?" She asked Trey and Dakota in a jokingly manner.

"We gotta wait for one to bite," Dakota replied. "It takes time, babe."

We sat there for what felt like forever, drinking, singing, and dancing before Trey finally got a bite. He reeled in a decent sized catfish and started rubbing his success in Dakota's face. The boys had made a bet earlier over who would catch the most fish that weekend, and so far, Trey was up by one. I was happy to see at least one of them catch something, but I had grown tired of sitting out there watching them reel in empty lines only to recast them. I congratulated Trey on his catch and then announced that I was going inside to take a shower and watch a little television. Apparently, I wasn't the only one ready to call it a night. The boys packed everything up, Heather put the fire out, and we all returned to the cabin.

The following morning the sun filled the sky, making

the view much more spectacular. Trey and I stepped out on the deck, and I became speechless as I gazed out at the lake. The way the distant mountains lined the water was beyond beautiful. Heather joined us on the deck, handing us each a cup of coffee. The three of us sat and watched Jet Skis and speedboats pass by while we waited for Dakota to wake up and join us.

The little boy and his father from the cabin next door were playing Frisbee on the little lake beach we had fished on the night before. The beach was directly in front of us, so it was entertaining to watch the two engage in their activity. His father would throw the Frisbee gently, only for it to fly right past the little boy every time. He seemed like a loving father, full of patience and determined to enjoy activities with his son. Each time the Frisbee glided past the little boy, he chuckled and chased after it.

The man eventually threw the Frisbee a little too hard, causing it to glide toward the deck we were sitting on. The little boy raced after it. As he came closer to the deck, he glanced up, noticing us sitting outside and froze. He just stood there, stiffly staring at us.

Trey quickly stood up to offer some assistance. He leaned over the deck and pointed to the Frisbee. "It's right there, buddy."

The little boy continued to stare in awkward silence.

"Need a hand?" Trey asked as he walked off the deck toward the Frisbee. Trey picked it up and handed it to the little boy. "There ya go, little man," Trey said in a gentle tone.

The little boy glared up at Trey and said, "There is a

65

monster with you."

"A monster?" Trey asked in a surprised tone, to play along with the child.

"Yeah," the child replied. "He's real big and scary."

Trey chuckled. "I bet he is! I bet he is a friendly monster, though."

The child glared up at the porch as if he were studying something. "I don't think so," he replied. "He says you need to be real careful."

"Oh." Trey continued to play along. "I wonder what he wants me to be careful about?"

"He said you shouldn't speak or look," the little boy finished just as his father called for him.

Trey stood in confusion as the little boy ran off to his father. When Trey returned to his seat on the deck, I asked what that was supposed to mean. I found it extremely odd that a random kid would say something so similar to the notes the neighbors had been leaving us. Trey shrugged and shook his head to suggest he had no clue what the child meant.

"It's a kid," Heather stated. "I'm sure he is just using his imagination."

"Why would he say 'don't speak and don't look,' Heather? You don't think that's odd?" I asked.

"I think it's a coincidence."

"Really? A coincidence?" I stated. "Before now, the only people that have told us not to speak or look are the neighbors."

"He is a kid!" She exclaimed. "We are miles away from the neighbors — it has nothing in common with them."

"She's right," Trey added, agreeing with Heather. "Let's not allow that to freak us out and ruin our time."

CHAPTER 5
HOME SWEET HOME

As depressing as it was to come home and face reality, every good thing must come to an end. We still had a week of spring break left, but since we'd decided to move away from campus, we couldn't afford to take off work any longer than a weekend. Responsibility called, and unfortunately, we had to answer.

College football was much different from high school; Dakota seldom had a day when he didn't have practice. Trey had to work, and Heather and I had plenty of homework that remained to be completed before classes resumed. Thankfully, I wasn't scheduled to work again for a few days, which I had requested. I liked to have a day or two to relax after vacation, as silly as that may seem. I know the entire point of a weekend getaway is to relax, but I always seemed to return home more exhausted, perhaps from having too much fun. Heather also had not purchased any new items for an entire weekend, which left her practically foaming out the mouth. She was beyond ready to return home so that she could check out the mall, and we were lucky enough to hear about her shopping plans all the way home from the lake. I was, however, very pleased to find everything at the house in the shape we had left it in. Nothing seemed to be vandalized, no animal carcasses awaited us, and no strange notes were left anywhere. It was like a welcome home gift from the neighbors.

Trey headed off to work, Dakota rushed to practice, and Heather and I unloaded our luggage and put things away from our lake trip. Once finished, she and I headed out on the town, stopping at a few stores and walking around the mall until my feet couldn't take anymore. Shopping with her may not have been my best choice, especially since she hadn't been able to do so in a few days. She had to make up for lost time, I suppose, but my muscles just couldn't keep up.

After expressing my agony to her on multiple occasions, we finally stopped at the food court inside the mall, where Trey and I both worked to rest for a moment. Upon arriving, we grabbed a seat at a small little table directly in front of Trey. He didn't notice us at first due to the line of customers waiting to place their orders. As I rested my feet, I couldn't help but watch him. He was the cutest thing in his uniform and dorky hotdog hat. I watched as he greeted and rang up customer after customer, using the same cheesy slogan each time. "Welcome to Big Dogs hotdogs, where the dogs are hot, and the food is fresh. How may I help you?" I couldn't keep myself from giggling a little each time he greeted someone.

Finally, when the line of customers disappeared, he came walking over to Heather and me with a hotdog in each hand and gave one to each of us, taking a seat next to me.

"Working hard, hotdog boy?" Heather asked. She took a tiny nibble from her hotdog.

Trey responded with a big grin on his face. "You know it."

Heather, who had locked herself out of her cell phone, handed it to Trey and asked him to take a look at it. He spent a total of three minutes messing with it and then slid it back to her, announcing, "All fixed." Anytime one of us had any issue with an electronic device, we knew exactly who to come to. Trey prided himself on his ability to fix technology, and it was definitely a skill he had that we all benefited from.

We chatted with him for a few more minutes until a customer came walking up and started scanning the menu. He kissed me on the forehead and jumped up. "Gotta go. I'll see you guys at home tonight."

We were about to leave the mall when we passed a sports store that caught Heather's eye. She claimed that she had been wanting to get Dakota a Pittsburgh Steeler's jersey for a while, but this was the first time I'd heard her mention it. She used any excuse to buy something new. My feet were so tired by then all I could do was fantasize about being at home and soaking in a warm bubble bath. I moaned and groaned to make my dissatisfaction known, but she insisted it would just take a moment and that we would be in and out. A moment to Heather could last a lifetime, and anyone that ever went shopping with her knew not to hold their breath whenever she was in a store.

We entered the store, and of course, she immediately darted for the women's clothing.

"You don't even like sports," I stated with an unpleasant look.

"I'm just looking," she replied, skimming through sports bras.

I huffed in frustration. I was not about to spend an hour in another store with her, especially since we had been out shopping all afternoon. I quickly sought out an associate and asked him where the Steeler's jerseys were located. Thankfully, this grabbed Heather's attention and forced her to return to our original mission. She purchased the jersey, and we left, but not without a strong attempt from her to go somewhere else first. On the way home, she negotiated with me to stop at one more place. Unfortunately for her, she was not a very good negotiator. I stood my ground well, and we went home.

I don't recall a warm bath ever feeling so good in my life. My eyes rolled in my head as I sank down into the bubbles. My legs had just started to relax when Heather entered the room, disturbing my peace. She had to use the bathroom and apparently didn't want to use the other one. She awkwardly sat on the toilet next to me. To make small talk, I asked her if Dakota was home yet, to which she replied that he had just called and was on the way.

"Let's watch a movie or something tonight," I suggested as she finished up and was starting to head out of the room.

She turned around to advise me that she would text Dakota and tell him to stop and grab a few movies.

"Nothing about dinosaurs this time, please," I added as the door shut behind her.

I must have dozed off in the bathtub because I was startled by a loud scream that forced my body to jolt and my eyelids to spring open. I sat in the tub for a few seconds in silence, attempting to resolve if I was possibly dreaming or if I really did hear something. As I sat there fully concentrated with my eyes slightly squinted, another loud scream echoed through the house — it was Heather.

I quickly stood up and exited the bathtub, dripping water all over the floor. I jerked my towel down from the shower rod, where I had hung it and draped it around my body before rushing into the hallway. As I headed down the hallway searching for Heather, another scream pierced my ears, but this time it was followed by a loud, "Stop!" My heart started pounding faster in fear that someone was harming Heather. Thoughts raced through my mind — could it be one of the neighbors? It wouldn't be the first time they broke into our home. What if Roberson or that creepy young man that never opened his eyes was hurting her? What was I about to walk in on? I was tempted to call the police, but Heather was in the other room, screaming, and I couldn't just hide and wait for help, allowing her to be harmed.

As I made my way into the living room to evaluate the situation, I saw Heather pinned down on the sofa by Dakota, who seemed to be tickling her.

"Get off!" She exclaimed, laughing uncontrollably. The two of them played around like that all of the time. Sometimes it was pretty annoying, but other times it was hilarious to watch them.

"You guys scared the heck out of me," I shouted, causing

both of them to stop what they were doing and focus their attention toward me.

Dakota appeared slightly confused as to why I was standing there in a towel with my soaking wet hair dripping all over the place.

"Sorry, I heard screaming," I announced. I quickly turned around to go get dressed.

"The only one sorry is Dakota," Heather stated as she grabbed a decorative pillow off the sofa and smacked him in the head with it.

"Oh, that's it," Dakota responded jokingly as he picked Heather up and body slammed her onto the sofa.

I slipped into my bathrobe. Screams and laughter echoed down the hallway and could be heard from the bathroom where I stood. Smiling, I gave my head a gentle shake. The two of them were like children at times but in the best way.

I returned to the living room and took a seat next to them. Dakota asked, "Ready to watch a movie? I got Jurassic World and King Kong." He tried to keep a straight face until Heather smacked him in the arm.

"No, you didn't!"

He laughed playfully. "Seriously, I picked out a few scary movies this time."

Trey had just called to tell me he was on the way home, so I wanted to wait for him to arrive before starting a movie. Heather went ahead and put the movie into the DVD player to have it ready while I made stovetop popcorn for the four of us.

When Trey came walking through the front door, he

greeted everyone and tossed his car keys on the kitchen counter. He walked up behind me and wrapped his arms around my waist.

"Making popcorn?"

"We're having a movie night," I replied.

He kissed my cheek and removed his arms from around my waist. "Oh yeah? What are we watching?" He asked.

"Who knows?" I answered. "Something Dakota picked out."

He told me that he was going to take a quick shower, which he desperately needed since he smelled like a hotdog.

"Hurry up," I replied. "The popcorn will be ready in a few minutes."

I divided the popcorn into two large bowls, one for Dakota and Heather and the other for Trey and me. By the time I was finished mixing the butter and salt into both bowls, Trey was finished showering. It never took him more than five minutes to take a shower — it took me longer to get undressed and achieve the perfect water temperature. He laid down on the sofa as I made my way into the living room carrying the two bowls of popcorn. I walked over to the recliner where Dakota and Heather sat cuddled up against each other and handed them their bowl. Then I trotted over to the sofa to lay down next to Trey.

The four of us munched on popcorn and watched the remake of Stephan King's IT. One part of the movie caused Heather to scream and jump, forcing her to spill popcorn all over the floor. She scared pretty easily, which Dakota and Trey often used to their advantage. The boys laughed at her when she got on her hands and knees and started cleaning up the popcorn.

"It's not funny," she declared. Even though I was far too invested in the movie to laugh, I'll confess it was pretty hilarious to see her jump like that. I demanded that they be quiet so that I could hear what was going on in the movie. To my dismay, my request only caused them to laugh harder.

Once the movie came to an end, I looked over and noticed Trey had fallen asleep. I don't recall a time that he ever managed to stay awake through an entire movie. As the credits began to play, I woke Trey up to tell him it was time to go to bed. He stretched for a moment. "Why'd you guys cut the movie off?"

Dakota chuckled a little. "Once again, you fell asleep halfway through, old-timer."

"Oh," Trey responded, still half asleep. "Was it any good? What did I miss?" We ignored his question since he was beginning to drift off again and instead instructed him to go get in the bed.

As we all said goodnight to each other, I noticed Dakota didn't stand up and follow Heather toward their bedroom like he normally did. Instead, he remained lounged back in the recliner with his arm behind his head, flipping through TV channels.

"Are you coming?" Heather yelled from the bedroom.

"I'll be there later," he yelled back. He continued to scan through the TV guide channel.

I had started making my way toward my bedroom. "Don't you have practice in the morning?" I paused to ask him.

"Yeah, but I'm waiting up tonight." He found a TV show he liked and selected it on the TV guide.

Remembering the promise he'd made to wait up until three to catch the culprit in our yard, I knew he was determined to remain true to his word. As much as I did not want him sitting up by himself, he insisted that he was going to stay awake that night, with or without us, just as he had planned to do before the lake trip. Eager to let it go and move forward, I contemplated how exhausted I was and explained that I had no desire to stay up late that night. I was still slightly sunburned from spending the past Saturday on the lake, and something about getting too much sun always made me want to sleep. Plus, shopping with Heather that day had completely drained me.

Dakota, who was too hardheaded to let anything go, made it known that he was going to wait up by himself, and nothing I could say would stop him. I didn't argue with him about it—the thought of him staying up actually made me feel a little better about being back at home. Even though his stubborn ways were problematic at times, it also made me feel safe in a strange way. He never had an issue with confrontation, and if any of us were to run an unwelcome guest off, it would be him.

Before heading off to bed, I demanded that he wake us up if he saw anything out of the ordinary.

That night I was far too exhausted to care about the neighbors. If they wanted to stand in our yard or plant stupid letters in our vehicles, so be it. I just wanted to sleep in peace. I left the blinds shut that night and made a point to seal the window curtains shut. I didn't care to see headlights or play any games with them.

I laid down next to Trey, who was sleeping peacefully and snuggled against him. It felt good to lie next to my boyfriend in the comfort of our own bed and not worry about unnecessary drama for once. A peaceful, carefree night like this one was all I really wanted. Determined to have that, I placed all thoughts about the neighbors in the back of my mind. I knew if anything were to happen that night, Dakota would take care of it, and at the very least, he would wake Trey up if something were to unfold.

I woke up the following morning feeling more refreshed than I had in weeks. It was like the weight of the world had been lifted from my shoulders. I made my way into the kitchen to get something to drink, where I was greeted by Dakota. His dark eye circles, poor posture, and sluggish energy showed he may have regretted his decision to stay up so late on a weekday. He was used to getting at least nine hours of sleep and didn't operate well on any less.

Regardless, he was pleased to announce that even though he had seen headlights, he'd seen no intruder in the yard last night. A sense of relief immediately flew through me. Was it finally over? The harassment we had endured since day one of moving into that house — had it finally came to an end?

As I stepped into my car that morning to head to work, I discovered there was no note waiting for me. I couldn't believe the neighbors would just suddenly stop bothering us, so I made a stop at the mailbox, and sure enough, there was no note in it either. I gained a sense of optimism when

Heather called to inform me she did not receive a note that morning, either. All we wanted was peace and a life where our biggest concerns revolved around paying rent, passing an exam, and winning a football game. Maybe we could finally have that. We didn't bother the neighbors at all and only saw them when we were pulling in or out of our driveway. We hadn't thrown any more parties at our house since it seemed Roberson didn't like a lot of noise. We didn't want to walk on eggshells just to keep peace with them, but we were willing to bend a little to keep the drama at a minimum. I thought it was finally over, and they were through with their constant scare tactics, but I could not have been more wrong.

That afternoon I arrived home to the smell of smoke and food in the air. The boys were cooking on the grill in the backyard. My empty stomach let out a loud rumble, and my mouth watered. Whatever they were cooking smelled amazing, especially since I hadn't eaten anything at work.

I could hear Heather screaming, "Is there a bug on me? Get it off! Get it off!" The sound of the boys' laughter followed her cries.

I rolled my car window up and stepped out with a big smile on my face. I stretched luxuriously, saying aloud to myself, "Home sweet home."

I turned to walk toward the back of the house to investigate what the boys were cooking. They must have heard me pull in because as soon as I turned the corner, Dakota popped out in front of me, yelling, "Boo!" I jumped back in shock and smacked him on the arm.

He giggled like a child for a moment. "You hungry? We're

grilling steak and potatoes," he said after getting the laughs out of his system.

"Mmm, that sounds amazing!" I exclaimed as I continued to walk toward Trey, who was flipping steaks on the grill.

I planted a peck on his cheek, and he asked, "How was work?"

"It wasn't too bad. Pretty slow today."

"Did you grab the mail on the way up?" He asked. "I think my cell phone bill is due."

I rolled my eyes and groaned, "I forgot to stop."

Heather, who was lounged back tanning in the afternoon sun, sat up and raised her sunglasses. "We can walk down and get it."

"Why don't you guys just take the car?" Trey suggested.

I quickly replied, "To drive what, fifty yards? We can walk down there — it won't kill us." It just seemed like a waste of gas to drive such a short distance. Besides, the air seemed to be cleared with the neighbors, so I didn't feel as nervous to walk down to the end of the driveway on foot.

Heather stood to her feet and accompanied me down the driveway. As we approached the bottom, I could see the neighbors sitting on their front porch like they always were. This time I tried not to pay them any mind and instead continued to chat with Heather. She didn't seem to mind their constant staring, and ignoring them was like second nature to her.

As I was removing the mail from the mailbox, Heather noticed a clothing magazine in my hand and eagerly jerked it away to start looking at it. There was always at least one magazine in the mail for her, and she could never wait to start skimming through them. Her credit cards always seemed to burn a hole in her pocket, and she took full advantage of every opportunity she had to use them.

While she stood there flipping through the catalog, I continued pulling out the rest of the mail. As I flipped through bill after bill, something caught my attention in the distance. A small object lying in the grass aligning the dirt road near our driveway glistened in the afternoon sunlight.

"What is that?" I asked Heather, pointing toward the shiny object. Heather glanced up from her magazine and squinted her eyes, searching for the object I was referring to.

"Right there," I stated. "You don't see that thing shining?"

When she finally spotted it, she stated, "Oh, that. Probably a beer can or something." She returned to her magazine as I approached the mysterious object.

I glanced over to notice the neighbors' eyes were still glued to me except for those of the young man, who sat with his closed. I ignored them and continued to close in on the shiny object. As I bent down and removed whatever it was from the brush on the ground, I noticed it definitely wasn't a beer can. It was far too small and flat to be any type of can. Besides, none of us hung around down there, and we certainly wouldn't toss our trash out like that. I wiped the dirt off the object in order to discover what it could be.

Upon realizing what it was, my heart skipped a beat. Startled, I dropped the object to the ground. My hands grew limp, and my disbelief must have been written in my face because Heather immediately closed her magazine and asked,

"What? What is it?"

As I stood stiff, attempting to process what my discovery could mean, Heather rushed over to me. She knelt down and picked up the piece of metal I had dropped, only to become just as shocked as I was. "We have to show the boys!"

"I'm sure there is a reasonable explanation," I said in a desperate attempt to return to a levelheaded state of mind.

"I'm sure there is," she replied. "But we have to show them."

I knew we needed to call the police because something that serious couldn't be overlooked, but I agreed with Heather. Showing Trey and Dakota what we'd discovered needed to happen before we did anything else.

We sprinted up the driveway, eager to show the object to Trey and Dakota. We bolted through the front door completely out of breath. Heather used what oxygen she had left to yell for them. Both Trey and Dakota came barging in through the back door, in a hurry to discover what the fuss was about.

As I began to explain, Trey removed the object from Heather's hand and held it up to study it. I could see the color leaving his face, and Dakota demanded him to hand it over so that he could evaluate it as well.

Dakota set the metal object on top of the kitchen counter. He paced back and forth with his hands locked behind his head, breathing heavily.

"Do you think it's real?" He asked, in search of some form of justification. "Maybe it's fake, and the neighbors planted it to mess with us." Dakota, like most people, wanted all problems to have simple solutions. He didn't handle it well when he couldn't make sense out of a situation.

As much as I disliked bringing him back to reality, I had to say, "If the neighbors were messing with us, they would've left it in one of our vehicles or something. Not hidden in the grass at the bottom of the driveway."

"We need to call the police," Trey joined in.

Without hesitating, Heather pulled her cellphone out and dialed 911 as we gathered around her to listen. We could hear the dispatcher's voice echoing through the phone speaker.

"Nine-one- one, state your emergency."

Heather looked over at me with a disturbed expression in her eyes and cleared her throat before responding. "We found a police officer's badge. I believe it may belong to a Rockwood officer that's been missing."

CHAPTER 6
THE NIGHTMARE NEVER ENDS

We woke up the following morning to discover the peace we'd thought we finally gained was short lived. The neighbors had graduated from planting paper notes around our property to spreading their message across the exterior of our home and down the sides of our vehicles. The words, Shh… don't speak and don't look, were spread across practically everything. We believed they used the blood from the four dead groundhogs we discovered on the porch that morning to write their message. Just like the rabbits we'd discovered, two of the groundhogs were missing their tongues, and two had their eyes removed. I wasn't even bothered by the gore from the sight anymore—it was something we were all growing used to.

Trey and Dakota washed the cars that morning while Heather and I scrubbed the house. We felt like we had reached a dead end, not really knowing what more we could do or where we could turn. Every time we reached out to the police for help, they didn't seem to take our situation seriously—

it always seemed to be a waste of time. Each time officers made an appearance at the neighbors' home, we were told the same thing. "No one is home." Despite the fact that we would see them sitting on their porch after the police left, we were treated like liars. After we handed the badge over to the cops, we were practically interrogated by them. No matter how many times we told them about the neighbors' tactics and how suspicious they seemed, they continued questioning us, almost like they thought we were hiding something.

We scrubbed the blood off our property in silence that morning—nobody laughed, nobody spoke, and nobody smiled. It was like the light at the end of the tunnel had vanished, and all optimism had left us. As much as I wanted this home together, I had started to regret our decision to leave campus. At least at Lincoln, I had peace of mind and wasn't greeted with animal carcasses every morning. I also never had to scrub blood off my items when I lived in Lincoln's dorm rooms. Sleeping next to Trey would've been nice under different circumstances, but I wasn't sure if it was worth it anymore at that moment. I enjoyed living under the same roof as Heather and Dakota and couldn't imagine my college years any other way. I began to think, what if we all left that house and found someplace else to live?

The rent was so cheap at the current house, which was one of the things that had drawn us to it, but surely we could find something just as cheap. Keeping a realistic attitude, I knew it would be extremely rare to find something as nice as that house for the price it was, but surely a downgrade would be worth it. When we first set out to find a place to rent, none of us had expected to find something so nice. Maybe we could return to our original expectations and settle for something else. A simple life that didn't involve constant conflict with neighbors was worth so much more to me than a nice home. Everyone seemed stressed and frustrated that morning, so I didn't share my desire to move. I thought it would be best to wait until later when everyone had a chance to cool off and recollect.

Once we were done scrubbing the blood off everything, Dakota headed off to practice, and Trey and I went to work, allowing Heather to tag along. She didn't want to stay at the house alone, and I couldn't say I blamed her. She declined an invite from Dakota to come watch him practice since she would rather spend her day at the mall. Trey made her aware that she would have to hang out at the mall for six hours until our shift ended, which only proved he had never gone shopping with her. Six hours was nothing for her to spend at the mall.

It was hard to concentrate on work that day as the thoughts of the police badge flooded my mind. We all wanted to believe Officer Taylor may have dropped it during his visit, but I think we each knew that was highly unlikely. It was more practical to assume that he'd lost it during some sort of struggle, but then again, he was a police officer with a gun. If Roberson had attacked a trained policeman, surely he would've been shot. And suppose the neighbors had done something to him—where was his police vehicle? You can hide a person a lot easier than you can hide something as large as a car. Then again, what if they dismembered the vehicle?

That would partly explain the pile of tires sitting in their yard. Maybe they were the tires from Roberson's victims!

The truth was, I didn't really know what to make out of the badge we'd found. The more I tried to make sense out of the situation and piece things together, the more confused I became. Just because we'd found a police badge across the street from the neighbors' home did not necessarily mean they did anything to Officer Taylor. I tried to keep my mind from jumping to conclusions, which wasn't easy. We had done our part by turning the badge over to the authorities, so it was up to them to investigate and analyze the situation further, not me.

We returned home that afternoon with a car full of shopping bags. It seemed when Heather was stressed, her addiction spiraled more out of control than usual. Trey and I assisted her by grabbing as many bags as we possibly could and carrying them inside. I attempted to talk to her about her addiction, only to discover it was a sensitive topic for her. She became a little snappy with me, insisting she did not have a problem, which forced me to drop my attempt to discuss it any further. Everybody needs a way to cope with life's problems, and I suppose Heather's outlet was shopping. Her parents didn't seem to mind since they continued to supply her with credit cards, so what business was it of mine? Deep down, I was just worried about her.

"Where do you want all this stuff?" I asked, attempting to smooth things over with her. She instructed Trey and I to place the bags on her bed so that she could put things away later.

After setting Heather's things down, Trey and I got in the shower together, which turned out to be a huge mistake. The entire time we fought over who was hogging the showerhead the most. It was definitely him! I couldn't even wash my hair without elbowing him in the face. Multiple times I instructed him to move out of the way, only for him to whine, "Fine! I'll just stand out of the water and shiver until you're finished." He was such a crybaby, but I couldn't help but find humor in his whining. As I was stepping out, he attempted to slide around me to get closer to the water stream, only to slip. In mid fall, he searched for a way to catch himself. Out of desperation, he grabbed onto the shower curtain, causing it to fall down on top of him. I don't recall a time when I laughed so hard in my life. We learned an important lesson that day; the two of us weren't meant to shower together.

As the night came to an end, Trey and I laid in bed watching television. I rested my head on his chest, lost in thought. I still hadn't expressed my desire to leave the house to anyone. As badly as I wanted to discuss it with Trey, I didn't want to keep bringing up drama. It seemed the neighbors controlled every aspect of our home lives, so when nobody was discussing them, I tried not to be the one to bring them up. I decided to keep the window blinds closed again that night simply because I didn't care to stay up and watch for headlights or catch anyone in the act of vandalism. What would it accomplish anyhow? I knew how it would play out if I were to see someone standing in the yard again. One of us would rush outside to confront the intruder, only for them to continuously whisper, "Don't speak and don't look." Afterward, they would disappear into the woods surrounding the property, like they clearly had done before. Nothing could be accomplished with those people. They were determined to bother us and practically lived to get under our skin. The last thing I wanted to do was submit to them and just sit back, allowing them to continue vandalizing our property. At the same time, I knew confronting them was pointless and only seemed to fuel their flame. I refused to give them the satisfaction of knowing their tactics worked. Instead, I placed it all in the back of my mind and drifted off to sleep.

Trey and I were later awoken by a loud scream. I quickly sat up in the bed and turned sharply to glance at the alarm clock—it was exactly three in the morning.

Trey, who was still half asleep, turned to me in a state of concern and asked, "Did someone scream? What was that?"

"I don't know," I replied as I motioned for him to be quiet so that I could listen out.

Another scream echoed through the hallway. Heather seemed to be in distress. Dakota was constantly messing with her, causing her to scream out, but not like this, and certainly not at three in the morning. This was obviously something serious; her scream was shrill enough to make me believe she was in real danger.

Without hesitating, Trey jumped out of bed and bolted toward the living room. I impulsively followed him, eager to discover what the commotion was about. I feared the worst. What could be causing Heather to scream out like that so early in the morning?

Once we made our way into the living room, I noticed

Dakota had been awakened by Heather's cries as well. He stood by the living room light switch in his boxers, suggesting he had just turned the light on. He appeared to be half asleep and in a state of confusion as he glanced around the room, attempting to discover what was going on. I walked toward the kitchen, where Heather lay in a fetal position with her head buried in her arms, sobbing. Broken glass from a drinking cup and ice cubes surrounded her on the kitchen floor.

Trey immediately scooped her into his arms and carried her to the living room sofa.

"What's going on?" Dakota asked, rubbing his eyes with the backs of his hands.

I had never seen Heather so upset. She sniffled from crying so hard and had a difficult time catching her breath. "Some-someone…. Someone…was in the house," she finally let out, with tears flowing down her face.

Heather began to cry hysterically as I rushed over and took a seat next to her on the sofa and put my arms around her. She buried her face in my chest and continued sobbing. Whatever she had seen had terrified her.

"Trey, can you sweep the glass up?" I asked, glancing up at Trey. He shuffled into the laundry room to retrieve the broom and dustpan and started cleaning the kitchen floor.

"Who was in the house, baby?" Dakota asked in a gentle manner. He sat down next to us and rubbed Heather's back.

"I-I don't know. He wa-was in the kitchen." We remained patient and kept trying to comfort her as she continued. "I got up to get a glass of water, and I saw him."

When she wasn't sniffling, I wanted to get as much

89

information out of her as I could. "Where was he standing?" I asked to gain a better visual image.

My question caused her to resume crying hysterically. Dakota continued rubbing her back and encouraging her to take her time.

"He wasn't standing. He was crawling through the kitchen with his mouth hanging wide open." An uneasy feeling came over me as I listened to her finish her description. "He just kept whispering 'don't speak,'" she cried. "I dropped my glass of water and just screamed as loud as I could."

"You couldn't tell who it was?" I asked eagerly to discover who was in our home. "Was it Roberson?"

"No," she cried. "It looked like he was wearing a police uniform or something." Dakota and I stared at her as we waited for her to continue. "It was so dark in here without the light on, but I think it was that officer."

Dakota wiped the tears away from her cheeks, helping her calm down.

"Officer Taylor?" I asked out of curiosity.

She nodded her head and cleared the lump from her throat. "I don't know for sure, but it did look like him. His eyes were closed, and his mouth was open. I could tell that much."

Trey, who had just finished putting the broom and dustpan away, joined us in the living room to suggest that maybe Heather was dreaming. She snapped back, insisting she was wide-awake and pouring herself a glass of water when it occurred.

"I know what I saw!"

I gently placed her hair behind her ears, removing it from her face. At that moment, I will confess I believed her mind was playing tricks on her. Officer Taylor would have no reason to come into our home unannounced like that. Besides, why would a police officer do such a thing? And where was the intruder if he had just been seen in the house? But regardless of whether she truly saw someone or not, she was very upset at that moment and needed reassurance from us.

To be on the safe side, Trey checked the doors to make sure they were locked. He wiggled each doorknob and declared that everything was locked up tightly.

"Baby," Dakota began in an attempt to help Heather return to reality, "The past few days have been stressful for us all. Maybe the police badge is on your mind, and being half asleep in the dark like that, you just thought you saw something."

Heather refused to allow any of us to convince her that she hadn't seen anything, and I wouldn't have attempted to do so. Instead, I continued to hug her and offered assurance by telling her everything was okay. By looking at her, I could sense her panicked state was transforming into anger.

"I want to leave this shit hole!" She yelled at the top of her lungs. "The nightmare never ends!"

Even though I kept trying to calm her down, I was glad she'd said that. I didn't want to be at that house anymore either, and it was relieving to hear I wasn't the only one. I glanced at Trey and Dakota as she continued to rant over how much she hated being there in that home. I wanted to make sure they were hearing her cries loud and clear.

CHAPTER 7
FIGHT FIRE WITH FIRE

We were all finally on the same page, desperate to get out of that house. The constant harassment had finally grown old to all of us, not to mention that Dakota and Trey were both tired of having to escort Heather and me everywhere. I refused to so much as go to the bathroom in the middle of the night without Trey by my side. Anytime Heather or I wanted a glass of water or a midnight snack, we woke the boys up and forced them to come with us. The reality that we were all miserable and slightly freaked out finally sank in. It was no longer worth the constant fight and tiresome mornings to remain in the hell we were living in. The neighbors were finally going to get exactly what they wanted—a life without us close by.

There was just one problem—we had signed a one-year lease, and the landlord didn't live in the same state as us. Our rent was paid by direct deposit every month, so we never really saw him. The only way of contacting him was through a phone number that seemed to only lead us straight to his voice mail. Eager to escape the house as soon as possible, we left voicemail after voicemail in hopes of hearing back from him.

We explored all of our options to get out of the house as fast as possible. We couldn't afford to rent anything else since our finances were tied up in the current place. We knew we would have to break our lease before we could start searching for something else to rent. The cheapest hotel around, which was well known for its roach infestation, was $75 a night. As terrified of bugs as I was, it would've been a joy to share a room with thousands of roaches compared to staying another night in that house.

The biggest issue was the financial aspect. Only five nights in a hotel room would've been more expensive than an entire month in the house, and we just couldn't afford that. The small amount of money Trey and I had saved up was spent during our lake getaway; we really didn't have the money to put out on a hotel room anyways. Heather could've covered it with her credit cards, but she feared that her parents would find out about her living situation. They apparently didn't know she was living with Dakota and somehow still believed she was staying at campus. She claimed they would take away all of her funds if they found out the truth, in an attempt to force her to obey their wishes. Out of desperation, we even considered going back to Lincoln's campus, only to discover they had boarded our old rooms out to other students. Our fate depended upon the landlord. I just hoped he would return our calls and be generous toward our wish to break the lease.

Day in and day out, everything was the same, almost like life was stuck on repeat. Every morning a surprise awaited us, and it was always the phrase, Shh...don't speak and don't look! either painted in blood someplace or written on a note and placed somewhere for us to find. It was like a demented Easter egg hunt every morning as we searched for what item the neighbors had vandalized. I imagined that's what hell must've felt like — living in a constant nightmare day in and day out, with no escape in sight.

When spring break came to an end, I think we were all thrilled. I was probably the first college student in history to actually miss going to class. Any excuse to get away from the house was welcomed, including sitting through a boring lecture. When I didn't have class or work, I spent my afternoons at a local coffee shop while the boys went to the gym across the street. The only time we were actually home was when we were sleeping or waking up to leave.

One afternoon while Heather and I sat at the coffee shop drinking chocolate mochas, my phone began to ring. I didn't recognize the number, and the area code hinted that it was a call from outside of the area. Curious to find out who the mysterious caller was, I answered the phone and was greeted with, "Hello, this is John Lynn with Lynn's Property Management. I'm returning your call."

I couldn't believe my ears; the landlord was actually on the other end of my phone after days of trying to contact him. I honestly didn't think he was ever going to call back, so I was quite surprised when he did. I pulled the phone away from my ear and covered the mouthpiece long enough to inform

Heather that he was on the phone. Heather, who was famous for background talking whenever anyone was on the phone, rambled on and on.

"Tell him we have to leave this week. Make sure you tell him about the neighbors. Oh, and don't forget to mention—"

I forced myself to ignore her so that I could concentrate as I began to explain our situation to the landlord. I expressed that we no longer wished to rent the property from him, but to my dismay, he didn't seem to handle the news very well. His tone completely transformed from chatty and warm to short and unpleasant. He put me on hold and took his sweet time searching for our contract in his database.

Heather kept asking me what was going on. She waved her hand in my face, paced in front of me, and tried pressing her ear against the backside of my phone. I finally informed her I had been placed on hold.

"Did you tell him about the neighbors?" She asked in an impatient nature. I nodded my head and signaled for her to be quiet. Heather sipped on her mocha and tapped her foot against the floor as she continued to wait impatiently.

Fifteen minutes later, the landlord finally returned to our call with devastating news. "It seems you guys signed a lease which clearly states you agreed to live in the property and pay rent monthly, for at least one year. You have barely lived in the home for two months, and already you want to break your contract?" His poor tone uncovered how frustrated he was by my request. I wasn't in the mood for an unpleasant conversation, but I tried my hardest to remain level headed as I explained the harassment we were enduring daily and how we were beginning to feel unsafe in the property. His response only showed how little he cared. "That sounds like something you should call the police over, not me."

My face became hot as anger pumped through my veins. "We have called the police," I said to him. "I know you can terminate our lease if you want, but I guess you are far too greedy and selfish to do that, huh?" I realize I should've remained calm since little is accomplished using anger. Given our circumstances, however, it was next to impossible for me to contain my rage.

"Ma'am," the landlord responded. "Everything I'm legally obligated to provide to ensure a suitable living environment, I have done. So unless you would like to go to court to push the issue, I will not terminate your lease because you are dissatisfied with your neighbors."

By that point, my anger completely got the best of me. I stood up from my chair and yelled into the phone. "Listen, asshole!"

Heather appeared to be shocked by my reaction. She started looking around the room and motioned for me to sit back down.

"We are victims of harassment on your property!" I continued. "I don't remember that being in the contract we signed, do you? You terminate our lease right now, or I will see you in court. Got that, scumbag?"

When the landlord didn't respond to my outburst, I removed the phone from my ear and so that I could glance at the screen, only to discover he had hung up on me. Upon looking up from my phone, I noticed everyone in the coffee shop, even the employees, was staring at me in awkward silence.

Heather, who nonchalantly sat in front of me sipping on her mocha, set her cup down on the table. She shook her head with irked eyes. "Didn't go too well, huh?"

I took my seat and filled her in on how horrible the conversation had gone.

"I'll take care of it," she declared, picking my phone up from the table. I figured it couldn't hurt to let her take a crack at the landlord, so I didn't attempt to talk her out of it.

She stepped outside to call him back, probably to keep from embarrassing herself like I just had. Not even five minutes later, she came storming back inside with a dissatisfied look on her face, just as I had expected.

"Didn't go too well, huh?" I asked in an attempt to mock her.

"That man is impossible!" She exclaimed, returning to her seat.

It was obvious that our landlord was not going to cut us any breaks, no matter how many times we called and begged. Neither of us could imagine being stuck in that house for an entire year, especially with the neighbors we were cursed with. The only plan of action I could come up with was to save for a lawyer and attempt to break our lease. With Heather unable to use her credit cards out of fear of her parents becoming suspicious, it was left to Trey and I to save the money. With rent, car payments, and all of our other bills, I knew it was going to be a while before we could afford to hire a lawyer. Every moment in that house was bad, but knowing we couldn't leave made our misery that much worse.

The bad news took a toll on all of us, but it seemed to impact Dakota the hardest. The next morning I was in the middle of scrubbing more bloody graffiti off the front door of the house when Dakota walked outside on his way to practice. As he approached his car, I made the mistake of asking him if he had a minute to help Heather, who was cleaning off the cars.

He completely snapped and began to pull his hair and kick the side of his vehicle. "I can't do this anymore!" He shouted with a hint of despair in his voice.

Heather dropped her rag and tried her best to calm him down. She wrapped her arms around him and said, "Don't let them break you, baby. We are going to get out of here soon."

Trey, who was on the other side of the house, scrubbing the graffiti that was left there as well, heard Dakota yelling and came running to help Heather and I calm him down. Neither of their tactics was successful. The dents he left along the side of his truck showed how serious he was. When he became enraged like that, it was next to impossible to calm him down. It took a lot for him to become that angry, but the neighbors made it look easy.

Dakota opened the chromed toolbox on the back of his truck and pulled out a can of spray paint. "If they wanna play, let's play." He started shaking the can back and forth to suggest he was mixing the paint up as he made his way down the driveway on foot. Trey, Heather, and I chased after him, attempting to stop him.

"Dakota! Dakota! Man, just stop," Trey yelled out. He

sprinted down the driveway behind him. "What are you doing?"

Dakota continued making his way down the driveway toward the neighbors' house. "They wanna ruin my things, then I'll ruin their things."

After that comment, I knew he was heading down there to spray paint their house, and honestly, I didn't blame him. The neighbors constantly vandalized our property; maybe it would be good to give them a dose of their own medicine for a change. The only reason I felt a need to stop him was because of Roberson—I feared what he might do to Dakota.

Eager to stop him, we continued to make our way down the driveway, in a hurry to catch up with him. To our surprise, when he approached the bottom of the driveway, he didn't act out his plan. Instead, he froze as if something had startled him. We kept yelling out to him, but it was like he was in a state of shock.

Once we caught up to him to see what his problem was, we each focused our attention toward the neighbors to see what he was staring at. It didn't take us a second to become just as shocked as he was. There was an extra person on their front porch that day, sitting right beside the young man on the steps. It wasn't a new face, however, Officer Taylor was sitting there with his eyes shut.

The four of us were confused, to say the least, as we stood there trying to process what we were seeing. Why was Officer Taylor sitting with the neighbors, and why were his eyes shut? Did they know each other or something? He focused his attention toward us, just like the young man had always done. It looked like they were staring at us through their eyelids. We stood there trying to make sense of it but couldn't come up with a reasonable explanation.

Trey stepped into the middle of the narrow dirt road between their house and our driveway and tried to communicate with the officer.

"Um, Officer Taylor?" He began, "What are you doing here?"

Officer Taylor sat there in silence, along with the rest of the neighbors on the porch. It was like he had become one of them or something.

Trey glanced back at us, hesitating for a moment before redirecting his attention toward Officer Taylor and continuing. "You know everyone is looking for you?" He cleared his throat and stood stiff, waiting for a response.

"That's the man I saw in the kitchen," Heather whispered to Dakota, nudging his arm.

I walked into the middle of the road, joining Trey. "Are you okay?" I asked the officer. "Do you need us to call someone?"

The young man and Officer Taylor immediately stood up, keeping their eyes shut, and started whispering simultaneously. "Shh...don't speak and don't look! Shh... don't speak and don't look!"

I stared at them in utter confusion, but they continued whispering the same phrase over and over. "Shh...don't speak and don't look!" The old lady's rocking chair creaked as she rocked back and forth ever so gently. I glanced around the porch, noticing each of them staring blankly toward Trey and me. Human behavior was the one thing I was passionate about, but I had never seen anything like this.

We stood there stunned, watching them for a moment and listening to the whispers until the wind began to blow hard. It ripped through the air, causing the trees around us to bend and snap about, and cold chills covered my body. I grabbed onto Trey's arm and cried, "Let's get out of here!"

The four of us sprinted up the driveway and bolted into the house. I bent over, placing my hands on my knees as I fought to regain my breath. "We need...we need to call the police," I suggested.

This was not something we could just ignore or take lightly. This wasn't a dead animal or a note; this was a police officer that had been missing for weeks.

"Sure, because they have been so damn helpful," Dakota said sarcastically.

I glanced around the room, expecting Heather and Trey to back me up, but to my surprise, they just stood there with their heads down. They couldn't possibly agree with Dakota.

"You guys can't be serious," I stated. "That man has an entire police station looking for him, for crying out loud. We have to report this."

Trey rubbed the back of his neck, refusing to make eye contact with me like he was about to say something I may not want to hear. "They practically interrogated us over the badge, like we knew something. Besides, the neighbors will just hide like they always do."

"He's right," Heather added. "They all but accused us of murder last time we called them."

I glared at the three of them in disbelief. I couldn't possibly begin to understand how any of them thought calling the police wasn't the best thing to do. "They clearly have him drugged or something, and you guys think that's okay? He's completely unresponsive, and he needs help."

Dakota chuckled like he had lost his mind. "Don't you guys see what's going on? The police are with them! That's why they lie for them and tell us no one is home every time. That's why Officer Taylor is over there right now sitting with them. They don't care about us. We are just a joke to them. Probably just one more group of people they made a bet on to see how fast they can make us crack."

I couldn't believe he actually believed his own words. "Dakota, you can't possibly believe the police are out to get us," I responded in an attempt to snap him out of his insanity.

"Fine!" He shouted as he pulled out his phone and tossed it to me. "Let's call them then. If that's what you want, go ahead, and let's see what happens."

It turned out calling the police was nothing more than a waste of our time. I made the call, and once the police arrived, everything went just as Dakota, Heather, and Trey had predicted. They claimed nobody was at the neighbors' and that it was highly unlikely that anyone lived there. They revealed to us that they went inside the property and searched it. No matter how many times I tried telling the officers that we had just seen the neighbors, they insisted nobody was there and threatened to fine us for filing false police reports, which was insulting, to say the least. One officer had the nerve to say, "I don't know what you kids are up to, but I will find out. I always do. Better hope your hands are clean when I do."

Even though the ideas Dakota had planted ran through my mind, I knew he was wrong. The thought of the cops plotting with the neighbors to harass us was just too crazy to believe. Thankfully, Heather and Trey both knew Dakota was being paranoid. Clearly, the neighbors were just hiding very well whenever the cops came knocking on their door. I was sure the police were very busy and received false reports often from kids with nothing better to do. For all they knew, we were just another group of college kids searching for some sort of entertainment.

Dakota may have been riddled with an insane suspicion, but he was right about one thing. He believed it was time for us to take matters into our own hands, and I agreed with him. Whether or not it was the wrong or right thing to do, one thing was certain — nobody else was helping us. Nobody made an effort to put a stop to the harassment and vandalism we received daily. And nobody seemed to care that we felt unsafe in that house. It was time to fight fire with fire.

CHAPTER 8
LET THE GAMES BEGIN

"So, what did you guys do?" Asked the sheriff with his gaze stuck on me.

I anxiously bit my fingernails. "We did what anyone in our situation would've done." I took a sip of water to calm my nerves. "We tried to kill them." I sat the cup of water down on the tabletop when my mind began to drift back to the events I'd survived....

***

Heather finally came clean with the real reason she couldn't help us pay for a lawyer or a hotel room. The story she gave us about her parents was just an excuse she had used to cover up something else. It turned out the stress from the neighbors had gotten to her, causing her shopping addiction to spiral out of control. She'd maxed out every credit card she had in a desperate attempt to temporarily escape her reality. I couldn't say I blamed her; if shopping would've buried my stress, even for a moment, I would've probably bought out a few stores as well. She was forced to come clean when we started pressuring her to use them. Her parents were going through a little financial trouble at the moment; it turned out addiction ran in her family. Her father had gambled their finances away and couldn't afford to pay off her credit cards at that time. Not that it mattered anyhow. We knew court would be a drawn out process, and a hotel room would've just been a temporary solution to a much larger problem we were faced with.

The four of us started plotting what we could do to stop the neighbors. Dakota suggested kicking Roberson's ass, which we all knew wasn't going to happen. Trey pitched the idea of investing in a security system, which would've been a great plan if we could've afforded one. Heather believed we could find friends to stay with, but unfortunately, our only friends were fellow students that had no room for the four of us. Those that did have the extra space were too intimidated by Lincoln's strict policies to risk it. We were left with no choice; it was time to fight back. We couldn't use our hands against someone the size of Roberson, so there was one option left—Dakota's gun.

Once we knew what we had to do, we came together to formulate a plan of action. Dakota explored the idea of just walking over to their house and dropping everyone, but we didn't want to harm anyone unless we had to. The goal was to stop the harassment, not go on a killing spree. Though we suspected Roberson, none of us really knew which one of the neighbors was responsible. Besides, Officer Taylor was innocent, and the last thing any of us wanted to do was shoot an officer of the law. We decided our target needed to be the individual causing the destruction.

It was agreed upon that we would offer a warning first and only resort to shooting someone if we absolutely had to. As much as I didn't like the thought of killing an individual, I knew something had to give. This person was vandalizing our property, breaking into our vehicles and our home, and killing animals. The neighbors were impossible to reason with, no matter how hard we tried. After seeing Officer Taylor in the trance-like-state he was in, it became clear that these people were potentially dangerous. They wanted to scare us, but we were through allowing it to work.

The question everyone had was, "How do we catch the culprit?" It was actually a very good question for which I had the answer. At exactly three every morning, I knew the headlights would cut on and gleam up our driveway like they did every night. In the past, those headlights had outlined a mysterious figure standing in our yard, which I knew was our suspect. The one time I'd tried to confront the individual, it didn't go very well, but with Heather, Trey, and Dakota on my side, I believed the four of us could handle it much better. Our plan was set. The four of us would wait by the living room window until three in the morning. Once the headlights cut on, if someone was revealed standing in the yard, we would rush outside to confront them and do whatever was necessary to stop them.

That day Dakota cleaned his gun, and Trey went out and purchased two No Trespassing signs. We nailed one of the signs to a tree at the bottom of the driveway and placed the other in our yard on a stake. The No Trespassing signs, along with our previous reports to the police, would hopefully justify Dakota shooting anyone if it came down to it. Heather made sure her cell phone was completely charged so that she would be able to film everything for evidence. If someone were to get shot, we wanted proof that they were warned to leave our property first.

I'll confess I was nervous and frightened over what was going to happen. A part of me believed it would be best to attempt to talk to Roberson one last time. But the other, more logical, part of me knew that approach wouldn't work. Whatever his reasons were, it was clear Roberson did not want us there and had no intention of stopping the destruction. Perhaps I was just trying to convince myself that we were about to do the right thing; I don't know. Regardless, I knew we were going to stick to our plan.

Early that morning, we gathered by the living room window. Trey kept a close eye on his watch, announcing the start of every new minute once two fifty-five approached. When he finally said it was two fifty-nine, Dakota loaded his gun and got it ready to fire as he announced, "Let the games begin."

Heather got the video recorder on her phone ready to film, while I quickly went around the room and cut every light off to prevent any glares on the glass window. I knew from my previous trials and errors that any light left on in the room would obstruct our view through the window, making it hard to see outside.

The four of us gazed out into the yard as soon as the headlights cut on. Sure enough, a figure was revealed standing there.

"That's definitely a person," Dakota declared. He bolted up from the sofa and stormed out the door.

We all followed behind him while Heather stood back and filmed. As soon as we stepped out onto the front porch, I just knew this was it, the moment we would end our nightmare. Now that I had everyone with me, we were finally going to catch our suspect in the act and put a stop to the destruction once and for all.

"Hey! I have a bullet with your name on it, buddy!" Dakota yelled toward the intruder.

The figure stood there in silence. Dakota held his hand out to us, motioning for us to stand back. He pulled his gun from his back pocket and steadily made his way off the porch to approach the figure.

"Do you hear me, asshole?" yelled Dakota, stepping closer but still keeping a safe distance from the suspect.

Heather, who had her cell phone pointed right toward the intruder, yelled out, "Just leave us alone!"

Right after Heather yelled out, the whispering began. "Shh…don't speak and don't look!" The whispering echoed through the air and sent chills through my body. The figure repeated, "Shh…don't speak and don't look! Shh…don't speak and don't look!" Dakota fired two shots directly at the individual just as the wind beat through my hair and the headlights cut off.

"Did you get him?" Trey asked hastily.

Heather cried hysterically.

"I think so," Dakota responded. He returned to the porch

to join us.

It was pitch black outside without the headlights gleaming into the yard, and the chill from the wind was unbearable. Before anyone could turn to open the door, the whispering returned, but this time it sounded much closer to us. "Shh... don't speak and don't look!" I clung tightly to Trey's arm as it came closer and closer. "Shh...don't speak and don't look!"

Heather jumped for the door only to discover it wouldn't open. "What the —?!" She cried. She pulled and pulled on the doorknob.

"Move!" Dakota panicked as he attempted to force the door open. He pulled and jerked with all of his strength, but the door wouldn't budge. It was like someone had welded it shut.

The whispering was coming closer and closer until finally, it sounded like the intruder was on the porch with us. I could not see my hand in front of my face, it was so dark out, but I could hear the presence of someone standing there with us. Their breathing was louder than the gusting breeze.

Trey swiftly removed the watch from his wrist and tossed it in the direction of the spotlight. His plan worked — the movement from the watch caused the spotlight to cut on. We peeped around only to discover nobody was standing there besides the four of us. Dakota jerked the door one last time, forcing it to swing open. In a state of panic, we scurried inside.

Dakota slammed the door shut and locked it behind us. He turned to us, with his back still pressed against the door. "Who...? What...? Who the hell was that?!" He blurted out in a state of confusion.

"I want to leave!" Heather cried.

I cut the living room light on to escape the darkness. Everyone rambled all at once, trying to make sense of what had just happened. I didn't know what to make of the event. How could someone be whispering to us one moment and be completely gone the next? Did Dakota shoot the suspect?

"Heather's phone!" I announced the second I remembered she had recorded everything. "We need to watch the video."

We gathered around Heather as she began to playback the video. We could see Dakota and hear his threats as he walked off the porch, but the distant figure wasn't showing up on the video. Maybe it was too dark, and he was standing too far away for her camera to pick up. We stood close to her, still watching the playback, and heard Heather scream, "Just leave us alone!" and the two shots fired. The video suddenly went dark, marking the point when the headlights cut off. We leaned in to listen closely for the whispers, but we never heard them. It was like the phone hadn't picked them up — but why? The wind was blowing very loudly, so I guessed that could've distorted the sounds of the whispers on the phone.

I woke up late that afternoon on the sofa next to Trey. We must have drifted off to sleep in the middle of our ongoing chatter about the neighbors. I lay there for a moment until Trey's obnoxious snoring beat into my ear enough to force me to sit up. I stretched and glanced around the room, noticing the television was still on from earlier that morning. Heather lay sound asleep in the recliner across from us, but where was Dakota?

I shook Trey and told him it was four-o-clock in the

afternoon. That news must have startled him because he immediately shouted, "What?!" as he rolled off the sofa and onto the floor.

"Relax," I said. "It's Saturday — we don't have work or class."

Our commotion forced Heather to wake up. She rubbed her eyes and started glancing around like she was searching for something. "Where's Dakota?"

I shrugged and told her that Trey and I had also just woken up.

"He's probably in the shower," Trey stated, standing up from the floor and untangling the blanket from around his legs.

A shower sounded like a brilliant idea, especially since I was drenched in Trey's sweat from sleeping so tightly against him. While I took a shower, Heather brewed a pot of coffee, and Trey got dressed and straightened up the living room. I don't recall a time when I ever felt so clean after a short shower. I don't know if it was because I slept the day away and needed to feel productive, or the fact that I'd woken up sticky and gross, but I felt like a brand new woman. I threw my clothes on and joined Heather and Trey in the living room. They sipped on coffee like it was morning.

"It's taking Dakota a long time in there," Heather stated. She placed her coffee mug on a coaster sitting on the coffee table. "I better go check on him."

Heather stood up from the recliner and stared at the television for a moment, suggesting she was invested in whatever she was watching. She eventually broke her concentration away from the television long enough to go check on Dakota. Trey and I continued to sip coffee and watch television until she came back into the room.

"He's not in there."

The creases in Trey's forehead displayed his confusion. "Huh, that's weird. Maybe he's outside." He set his cup of coffee down and stood up to make his way out the front door.

"He's probably checking the yard over for blood or something," I said to Heather to remind her of the chaos we'd endured earlier that morning.

She returned to her seat and leaned toward the television to continue watching whatever she was so invested in. It appeared to be some sort of lifetime show. You know, the typical movie where a woman defeats a bad guy and feels completely empowered in the end—that type of show. Heather loved movies like that no matter how cliché they were, the suspense always seeming to keep her on the edge of her seat. Dakota would always tell her, "Once you've seen one of those movies, you've seen them all." But she never seemed to listen to him. Anytime someone would speak when she was watching one of those shows, there would be hell to pay. She took it very seriously and expected everyone in the room to do the same, or to at least remain silent until a commercial came on. Trey and Dakota always gave her a hard time by pretending to cough and sneeze really loud during the best parts just to annoy her. Even though I always sided with her and told them to stop, I secretly found it to be hilarious. They always knew how to push her buttons and get her going, and she never was too good at ignoring them.

I made myself comfortable and sipped my coffee in silence until Trey finally came walking back in through the front door. He started taking his shoes off. "I didn't see him anywhere. But his truck is here, so he has to be around here somewhere."

None of us really thought much of it at that moment. Dakota rarely sat still when he was awake, so I just assumed he was out gathering firewood or something. Trey, Heather, and I had slept all day, and none of us could really blame Dakota for not wanting to sit around and waste his day waiting on us.

Hours passed, and daylight gradually faded, but there was still no sign of Dakota. We were starting to grow slightly concerned over his whereabouts.

"Maybe we should call him," I suggested to Heather.

"I already have a few times. He isn't answering," Trey stated.

Heather stepped out on the porch and yelled for him, only to receive no reply. My concern grew in strength as questions flooded my mind. Where could he be? Why wasn't he answering his phone?

I joined Heather on the porch and listened to her call his name once more. "Dakota!"

"Maybe one of his football friends picked him up. He might be at the gym."

"No. He would've told me he was leaving." She pulled out her cell phone and dialed his number.

I knew she was right; Dakota wouldn't have left without telling someone. But then again, we had been asleep. Maybe he didn't want to wake us up. He had been known to spend all day at the gym working out. It wouldn't have been the first time one of his friends picked him up to go to the gym, either. He also kept his cellphone in a locker during his workouts, so that would explain why he wasn't answering.

My thoughts were interrupted when I heard a faint ringing sound coming from the distance.

"Do you hear that?" I asked. I made my way off the porch to follow the ringing. When the ringing stopped, I instructed Heather to keep calling Dakota. I walked into the middle of the front yard, trying to locate the source of the sound. As I searched around the yard, I eventually realized it was coming from the woods surrounding our driveway.

"Keep calling," I demanded as I stepped into the woods.

The wooded area was so thick it was challenging to form a path through in order to go toward the ringing. Sticker briar bushes tore through my skin and tangled their way into my hair as I fought to make my way through. I called Dakota's name time and time again but received no answer.

"Hurry up, Leah!" Heather called out from the porch. "It's getting dark!"

"Just keep calling!" I yelled back. I continued fighting my way through the brush, getting torn to pieces by sticker briars and tree limbs.

I eventually forced my way through toward the ringing. As I stood there, right where the ringing was coming from, I looked around and saw no trace of Dakota. I glanced down at my feet, where I discovered Dakota's cell phone laying there under the dead leaves. I crouched down to pick the phone up and noticed something far more troubling. Right beside his phone lay his pocketknife, covered in blood.

CHAPTER 9
HELLO? WHO IS THIS?

The night grew cold, but there was still no sign of Dakota. Trey called everyone he could think of that might know where he was but to no avail. The three of us checked the gym, football stadium, and every other place we could think he'd be. I couldn't bring myself to mention the bloody pocketknife I'd found next to his cell phone to Heather. She was already worried sick—the last thing she needed was to believe something terrible had happened to him. I needed everyone to remain as calm as possible so that we could search for him together with clear minds. After seeing Officer Taylor in the state he was in, I feared the neighbors had done something to Dakota. I didn't want to jump to conclusions, even though I knew Dakota wouldn't have ventured off into the woods like that. And he certainly wouldn't have dropped his cell phone and left it behind. The blood on his knife and the way the leaves on the forest floor were scattered about made me believe there had been a struggle of some sort. Did Dakota attempt to confront Roberson that day? If so, did it go horribly wrong? We had to find him.

Even though the police hadn't been the least bit helpful in the past, we needed to speak to them. My friend was out there somewhere, and I had a horrible feeling in the pit of my stomach that wherever he was, he was in trouble. The three of us drove down to the Rockwood County police department with the hopes of getting their help in finding Dakota. By that point, most of the officers already knew our faces. When we were telling the entire department that our friend was missing, one officer spoke up.

"Okay, slow down. Why don't you kids come with me to my office and tell me what's going on?"

We followed him to his tiny office in the back of the building, where he instructed us to have a seat. I don't think he realized there were three of us because there were only two chairs in the room. To make it work, Heather and I shared a seat while Trey situated himself in the other.

The officer stood in front of us in an unwelcoming manner with his arms cross. "Okay, now one person at a time, tell me what's going on."

One at a time, the three of us blurted out details explaining to the officer that Dakota was missing. We described what happened that morning when we confronted the intruder in the yard, and I told him how I found Dakota's cell phone laying in the woods.

The officer wrote us off with explanation after explanation. "Maybe your friend just took an afternoon stroll." It soon became clear by his lack of concern that he wouldn't be much help. I don't know why we bothered going in there that night to start with. I guess a part of me believed the police would care this time and actually do their jobs and help us.

"He wouldn't do that," Heather declared, unwilling to give up.

The officer's phone started ringing, but instead of ignoring it and continuing to focus on us, he asked us to hold on a moment and answered it. He stepped out of the room as he carried on his conversation with whomever.

I glared at Trey and shook my head in disbelief.

"Maybe it's something important," Trey whispered.

At that time, we heard the officer through the door as he spoke to his caller. "So, what's for dinner tonight?"

As unbelievable as his mannerisms were, all we could do was sit there and wait for him to hang up the phone and return to the room. At the very least, he could've pretended to care about our situation. My friend was missing, yet it seemed the authorities were not taking us seriously.

The officer finally returned to the room and apologized to us for the inconvenience. At least he was good at faking apologies.

"Now, where were we?" He began. "Oh yeah—your friend hasn't been home in a few hours."

His mannerism was insulting by then. I didn't want to upset Heather more than she already was, but I had no choice but to inform the cop about the pocketknife. Maybe that would spark a little sympathy and force him to take our situation more seriously.

"I didn't just find his cell phone," I admitted. Trey turned to me with a dumbfounded expression. I took a deep breath.

"I found something else that makes me believe Dakota might be in trouble." This, of course, grabbed the officer's attention, but unfortunately, it gained Heather's focus as well. "I also found his pocketknife laying there, covered in what appears to be blood."

I removed the knife from my pants pocket, where I had placed it and handed it over to the officer. He briefly studied the knife while Heather started sobbing. I'll never forget the look she gave me after that. It was a look that made me believe years' worth of friendship had suddenly ended. She stood up and stormed out of the room. I hung my head in shame once I noticed the look of disappointment on Trey's face.

"Why didn't you tell us?" Trey asked, staring right at me unbelievingly.

I took a deep breath without looking up at him. "I didn't want you guys to get upset and jump to conclusions. I was trying to protect you both." I knew I was wrong to hold information like that from them, but my intentions had been pure. I honestly didn't want either of them to dwell on the idea that something terrible might have happened to Dakota. He was the love of Heather's life and practically a brother to Trey. I loved him too. He was like the big brother I never had, and the thought of something bad happening to him completely destroyed me inside.

"Well, thanks." Trey sounded angry. He jolted to his feet and shook his head in disappointment. "Thanks for deciding what's too much for me to handle." He stormed out of the room after Heather.

I stared at the floor and fought to hold back my tears. The

officer sat down in the newly available chair Trey had been sitting in. He leaned toward me to finish our chat. "You think this is his blood?" He asked, holding up the pocketknife.

"I don't know," I responded. "I hope not."

The officer tossed the pocketknife onto a small desk in the corner of the room. He tapped his fingertips together like he was thinking deeply about something. "And you say you believe the neighbors might have done something to him?" He continued to tap his fingertips together, glaring smugly at me over his long pointed nose.

I nodded my head. "Yes. Yes, I do."

"Okay." He stood up and adjusted the belt around his plump waist. "You kids wait here, and I'll grab backup and go check everything out."

Once the officer had left, I knew I needed to go find Trey and Heather. I just didn't know what to say to them to ease the tension. They had every right to be upset with me, and I didn't blame them for it. If it had been Trey missing instead of Dakota, I would've been hurt if Heather kept something like that from me. I just hoped they would eventually understand that I only did it because I wanted to protect them from something so worrisome. When I first saw the knife and the blood, I feared the worst. I didn't want them to feel the same way. I just hoped they could forgive me, and the three of us could move forward and find Dakota. No matter what, I couldn't bring myself to lose hope. I just knew Dakota was out there somewhere, alive and waiting for us to find him. That needed to be our main focus, not a pocketknife. For all any of us knew, it could've been someone else's blood on that knife. Dakota may have stabbed one of the neighbors in self-defense or something. I couldn't allow my mind to consider otherwise. We had to remain focused if we wanted to find him.

I sat in that tiny office, alone with my thoughts, for about twenty minutes before I gained the courage to go look for Heather and Trey. I hoped by then, it had been long enough for them to forgive me, and we could focus on what was more important, finding Dakota. I stood up from the chair and made my way toward the exit of the tiny office when my phone began to ring. I removed my cell phone from my back pocket and glanced at the screen, expecting to see Trey or Heather calling, but it wasn't. My legs trembled like jelly, forcing me to return to my seat when I saw who was calling.

Thinking I must be seeing things, I closed my eyes and reopened them, only to see the same thing. It had to be some sort of sick joke or a glitch in my phone because it wasn't possible. The phone finally stopped ringing when I put it on my lap. I couldn't process how something like that could happen. As I picked my phone back up to check it for water damage, it started ringing again. The screen read, Incoming call: Dakota. But how was he calling me? I was sitting at the police station staring at his phone lying on a desk in front of me.

I stood up and walked toward the desk where Dakota's phone was laying. I slowly picked it up to evaluate it, only to discover it was turned off. After the ringing stopped, I turned Dakota's phone on. The screen lit up, revealing his wallpaper, which was him and Heather standing on a beach. My phone started to ring again, but this time I was staring right at Dakota's phone, which wasn't calling anyone.

I dropped his phone back on the desk and answered mine, holding the speaker against my ear and staying quiet. At first, all I could hear was a bunch of static until a voice faded in. It was impossible to make out what they were saying through the static.

"Hello? Who is this?" I asked.

The static continued for a moment until the words, "Shh... don't speak," broke through clearly.

"Who is this?" I demanded to know once more.

I stood there, listening to the static until the caller hung up. I promptly redialed the number, only for the phone sitting on the desk in front of me to start ringing. It made no sense. How did Dakota's phone dial me, and who was on the other end?

I needed to find Heather and Trey; maybe they also received a strange call from Dakota's number. I dashed out of the police station and into the parking lot, where I noticed the light was on inside of Trey's vehicle. As I approached the car, I could see Trey and Heather sitting inside. Upon walking up to the passenger side of the car where Trey was sitting, the two of them glared at me. Pieces of Heather's hair were sticking to the sides of her face from where she had been crying. The two of them stared at me in silence as if they were waiting for me to say something.

"The officer went to check things out," I said, breaking the awkward silence.

"We know," Trey replied curtly, staring at the floorboard.

I stood next to the car in silence with my head down until Trey stepped out and opened the back door, motioning for me to get in, so I did. The stillness that fell amongst us during that moment was the loudest thing I've ever heard. Trey sat there in the passenger seat with his head down, like he was lost in deep thought. Every once in a while, he would close his eyes tightly and reopen them, as if he were trying to rid his mind of an unwanted idea. Heather had leaned her head against the driver's side window and just gazed out into the half empty parking lot. It was hard to say where her mind was with everything going on, but her trance-like state told me it wasn't in the car with her. I imagined she was thinking about Dakota, probably searching for answers to the same questions I was asking myself. Where was he? Was he safe? Was he hurt? Were the cops having any luck with the neighbors this time? How much longer would we have to sit there and wait for them to return to the station?

"Listen, guys —" I began before Heather interrupted me.

"It's okay, Leah," she muttered with her head still pressed against the window.

At that moment, I don't know what came over me. Everything I had been holding in came rushing to the surface, and I couldn't hold back my tears any longer.

"It's not okay!" I cried. "I just want him to come home! But I'm sorry I didn't tell you guys everything." The tears flowed down my face as Heather turned around and stuck her hand out toward me. I placed my hand in hers, and she squeezed it tightly.

"I know he's okay," she assured me. "He'll come back

123

home."

Trey glanced back at me and nodded his head with a half drawn smile. I wiped my tears away and smiled at the two of them. I leaned in and hugged Heather tightly. I didn't know what would happen or when Dakota would return, but I did know the three of us had to stay strong and stick together.

I sat back in my seat. "Did you guys get a strange phone call?"

Both of them shook their heads and looked at me expectantly, suggesting they had no idea what I was talking about.

"Just a few moments ago, I got a call from Dakota's number." I pulled my phone out to show them my call history. To my surprise, there was no record of Dakota's call anywhere on my phone. I frantically searched through my missed and received calls, but nothing was there to suggest his number had called me. "I swear!" I exclaimed. "His number called me multiple times...."

The two of them glanced at one another as if they believed I had lost my mind. "That's impossible," Trey snapped. "We handed his phone over to the police, Leah."

Eager to make them believe me, I continued to stress my case. "I know. I know his phone is in the police station sitting on the cop's desk. Listen, guys, it sounds crazy, I know, but someone really did call me from his number, I swear."

Trey sighed deeply. "I think we are all just worried right now, and our minds are beginning to wander. Let's not do this right now, though, okay?"

I knew my mind wasn't wandering. Sure, I was worried,

but I wasn't going crazy. Someone out there was able to make Dakota's number pop up on my phone. I didn't know who had done it or how, but I knew what I had seen and heard. But I didn't want to drag it on any further since it seemed to upset Trey and Heather. Plus, no matter how much I stressed to them that someone had called me, they weren't going to believe me. So I let it go.

The silence returned as we sat there in Trey's car, waiting for the officer to return. I could only hope he had been gone for so long because he found the neighbors. I had told him about the way they hid every time the cops showed up, so maybe he was looking extra hard this time.

Minutes had passed when Trey's phone started to ring. When he picked it up to look at the screen, the color disappeared from his face. The way his eyes grew twice as large and the way he sat there speechless was almost like he had seen a ghost. I didn't need to ask because I already knew who the caller was. Heather, on the other hand, was curious to discover why he suddenly appeared so distraught. She leaned over to take a look at his phone and gasped when she saw Dakota's number on the screen.

Trey hesitated a moment before he answered. I leaned in from the back seat once he put the call on speakerphone for all of us to hear. As the static echoed through the speaker, Heather anxiously lowered her head toward the phone and said, "Hello?" The static continued muffling the speaker while Trey stared at me in disbelief.

"Hello? Who is this?" Trey asked nervously.

Through the static, we soon heard the words, "Shh…don't

speak and don't look!" It sounded just like the whispers we'd heard in the yard the morning we tried catching our intruder.

"Who is this?" Trey stressed once more before the caller hung up.

As he slowly lowered his phone, Trey appeared to be shook up. He gulped and twisted his fingers. Heather, who was just as bothered by the call, glanced at me as if I knew something. I wished I had answers for her, but the truth was I was just as confused over the strange call as they were. Trey frantically skimmed through his call log, only to discover the same thing I had; there was no record of the call left behind whatsoever.

As Trey continued searching his phone for an explanation, we were all startled by a loud "Bang! Bang!" Heather screamed, and I jumped when the officer surprised us by tapping on her window with his flashlight.

The three of us stepped out of the vehicle to address the officer.

He apologized for sneaking up on us. "Just wanted to let you kids know my partner and I went and checked everything out. I didn't see any trace of your friend."

Trey scratched the back of his neck, continuing to examine his phone. The officer must have sensed our disconnection because his expression grew concerned. "Is everything okay?"

Heather shook her head before responding. "Where is his phone?"

"I told you," I said. "It's on his desk turned off." I pointed at the officer.

Heather stormed off. The officer appeared to be more

confused than ever by her mannerisms as he watched her burst through the entrance of the police station.

"Whoa!" the officer exclaimed. "What is she doing?" His smug face was pointed at the station.

Before we could explain, he fled off after her. I jerked Trey's arm to break his concentration away from his phone and pulled him along with me as I sprinted after them. Once we entered the office, Heather was in the process of cutting Dakota's phone on when the officer demanded an explanation.

"He called us!" Heather anxiously stated without so much as looking up at him.

The officer's eyes wandered around the room as he stood there, trying to process Heather's statement. "Who called you?" He asked, motioning for her to calm down.

"Dakota! Dakota's cell phone called us!" She exclaimed as the phone powered on.

The officer shook his head and said, "That's impossible. That phone has been sitting safely in my office."

Heather ignored him and continued to inspect Dakota's phone, determined to figure out what was going on. Trey approached her and started looking the phone over as well.

"I know it sounds crazy," I said. "But this phone did call us."

The officer removed the phone from Trey's hand and began to look through it. "Says the last call made from this phone was yesterday."

We had no way to prove to the officer that someone called us from that phone. Since the number was not showing up in our call logs, we appeared to be nothing but a few crazy kids as far as he was concerned.

"You can't just run into my office without permission like that," the officer bickered. He gave Heather a stern look.

She hung her head and closed her eyes in defeat. I suppose she knew nothing she said would make the cop believe her.

"So, what happened with the neighbors?" Trey asked in an attempt to change the subject and also unravel answers.

"Well, I can tell you right now it doesn't seem to me like you kids even have neighbors," the cop uttered. "My partner and I went inside of the home, and nobody was there. Seems like it's just an old abandoned shack to me, certainly no home."

I shook my head furiously. There was no way I was going to stand there and allow another police officer to tell me, "Nobody's home," and leave it at that. "They are hiding from you!" I lashed out.

"Ma'am'," the officer began. "We searched the entire premises from top to bottom. If someone was hiding, I can assure you we would've found 'em."

I couldn't believe what I was hearing. My friend was missing, and Trey and Heather were devastated, yet the police acted like they had reached a dead end and couldn't do anything more. Every time we called them, it was the same excuse. Yet as soon as they left, we would see the neighbors sitting right there on the front porch like always. It was like I had entered The Twilight Zone as I stood there in the police station that night. When would it end? When would the police finally do their job and help us? Were the neighbors going to continue getting away with everything just because they hid when the cops came knocking?

As I stood there with my brain racing, a thought hit me. The neighbors hid from the police, but they never hid from us. "Come with us!" I fired off to the police officer. "Ride with us, and I will show you they are home. I'll also take you to Officer Taylor."

The police officer chuckled as if something I said was funny.

"No," Trey firmly said. "That's actually a genius idea! Every time you guys leave, they return to their front porch. If they don't see your police car, I bet they wouldn't think to hide."

The officer huffed and shook his head. "Look, I'm very busy. I don't have time to keep running in circles with you kids tonight."

We continued to go back and forth with the officer, but we weren't convincing enough. Nothing we said would force the officer to change his mind and just ride with us to the neighbor's house. The look on his face made it well known that he didn't believe a word we were saying.

"In twenty-four hours, give us a call if your friend isn't home yet. You can file a missing person's report then," the officer concluded as he held his office door open and waved us out.

On the way back to the house that night, I found myself losing all hope. I stared out the window and thought about Dakota, wondering if he knew we were looking for him and if he was scared or hurt. As unfortunate as it is, you don't realize how much someone means to you until something terrible happens to them. I could only hope, wherever he was, he knew the three of us would never give up. We would never stop searching for him and never stop praying to hear his voice again. I didn't know who the caller was that managed to make his number show up on our phones, but it was clear; someone out there knew something. Whoever was showing up in our yard, vandalizing our property, and leaving notes for us to find had done something to Dakota. There was no doubt in my mind that the neighbors were responsible, but how could we prove it? How could we convince the police that they were inside of that house hiding somewhere?

As we approached our driveway, Trey slammed on the brakes, forcing the car to come to a halt. I jumped to see why he had stopped so suddenly.

"There they are," he muttered as he glared toward the neighbors' house.

I glanced over, and sure enough, they were all sitting on their front porch. The old woman, the little girl, the middle-aged woman and her baby, the young man with his eyes closed, and Officer Taylor.

Heather became enraged as she opened the car door and yelled out, "Where is my boyfriend?" Even in the middle of the night, I could see the red in her face. "If any of you fucking touch him, I will kill every last one of you!"

Trey interrupted her screaming session, telling her to relax and get back inside of the vehicle.

Instead of listening to him, she continued to yell. "Do you hear me? You deaf assholes! I know you did something to him, and we turned all of you in to the police!"

Their front door swung open, and out walked Roberson.

Without saying a word to us, he ambled toward the car.

Heather stood stiff, still yelling and cursing, "Where the hell is he?! Answer me!"

As Roberson came closer, I noticed what appeared to be hedge clippers in his hand. I wasn't quite sure why he was holding the tool and what his intentions were.

Trey must have noticed what Roberson was carrying as well because he immediately panicked. "Heather! Get in the car now!"

Once she saw Roberson heading toward her, holding the hedge clippers, she swiftly returned to her seat and slammed the door shut. Trey stepped on the gas pedal, spinning tires up the driveway. Once we reached the house, he whipped the car into the back yard so that we would be right next to the back door. We rushed inside and locked the door behind us.

"What was his deal?" Trey stressed with wide eyes.

"I'm not sure," I replied. "Was he trying to attack us?"

"Yes!" Heather shouted. "He's insane!"

CHAPTER 10
WHAT HAVE YOU DONE!

Days had passed, and there was still no sign of Dakota. The search for him had spread massively. It covered the local newspaper and was broadcasted all over Rockwood's news channel. His parents even went public and offered a reward for anyone that had any information on where he may be. Lincoln hosted a ceremony on his behalf to raise money for the family, and the entire football team painted his jersey number on the sides of their helmets in his honor. Everything felt depressing, almost like the life had been stolen from everything once grand. It was like a dark cloud hung over the top of Rockwood as the search for Dakota continued, but nobody was ready to give up. The community came together in every way possible to express their sorrow. Professors grieved, and fellow students hung their heads in disbelief.

Perhaps the individual that suffered the most was Heather. She was completely broken by the tragedy. Though Trey and I were also devastated, we tried to stay strong for her.

I remained positive on the outside, but inside there was a completely different story to tell. The hope I had about Dakota returning had vanished once reality sat in; Dakota wasn't coming back, at least not in the same shape as when he'd left. I didn't know what happened in the woods the day he disappeared, and I had to face the reality that I never would. Even though I felt hopeless, I couldn't let Heather sense that. Trey and I were eager to do everything we could do to keep her spirits high, even if that meant faking a smile.

Trey, Heather, and I knew the neighbors had done something to Dakota, but we didn't know what. Just like they did with Officer Taylor, those people had a way of making others vanish without a trace. And if they did reappear, they wouldn't be the same person they were before disappearing. Everyone that stood on that porch seemed to be in some sort of trance-like state like they were hypnotized or something.

We suspected Roberson was drugging individuals and holding them hostage for unknown reasons. How else could Officer Taylor's condition be explained? He was stuck on that porch, nearly lifeless, where he blended in with the others that sat alongside him. He certainly wasn't the same man we'd spoken to that day in our driveway. He'd disappeared as a functional human, only to reappear as a shell of a man.

But what could we do about it? We couldn't even prove that the neighbors existed, much less that they had done something to Officer Taylor and Dakota. Authorities had searched the property in response to our claims multiple times, only to find nothing. No matter how much we stressed to the authorities that the neighbors were hiding from them, we weren't taken seriously. Instead, Trey, Heather, and I became the lead suspects, and it wasn't just the police that believed we were behind it all.

Only a few people in town would so much as make eye contact with us. Anytime we went out for any reason, we were haunted by whispers, slurs, and the judgmental stares of townspeople. Everyone at school treated us as if we had a scarlet letter branded on our foreheads. The poor treatment at school didn't last long, however, because we were eventually suspended while the investigation was going on. So much for innocent until proven guilty. Dakota's parents refused to speak to us when we tried to reach out and express our condolences. We were left with nobody to turn to but each other.

Desperate to find a solution to our never-ending problem, we turned to the community for answers. We sought out information about Roberson from the few locals that didn't have us labeled as demented killers. Strangely enough, nobody seemed to know who he was. Everywhere we turned was nothing more than a dead end. There was something so mysterious about the neighbors. The way they managed to hide in the shadows and avoid everyone in the community was beyond me. Nobody knew them, and the police didn't even believe they were real. It was like we were the only people in the world that knew they existed. I didn't know how they managed to stay so secretive or what their game was, but we owed it to Dakota to find out.

Trey decided to confront Roberson one more time, but Heather and I refused to allow it. The night he had approached us carrying the hedge clippers was just too strange for comfort. He was a dangerous man, and if he were to harm Trey, there would be nothing Heather and I could do about it. We had to be smart if we were going to expose them and bring justice to Dakota and Officer Taylor.

Heather came up with a brilliant idea to prove our case to the authorities. We would use video evidence and show the police pictures and recordings of Officer Taylor sitting there on that porch. That would've been the easiest way to gather our proof, but there was just one problem — Trey.

Trey wanted nothing more to do with the police after they accused us of Dakota and Officer Taylor's disappearances. I certainly understood his point of view; the police had practically ruined our lives. We were grieving over our friend, yet they turned us into the most hated people in all of Rockwood. Trey thought turning to them again would only make our situation more difficult. But Heather and I knew we needed them on our side if we were to ever get to the bottom of things and find out where Dakota was. We needed Roberson to talk, but first, we needed the police to believe us.

Heather and I came up with a plan of action. First, we would call the police and have them on the way. That would give us about twenty minutes to drive down to the bottom of the driveway and snap a few pictures of the neighbors. Once the police arrived, we could then show them the evidence, and they would have no choice but to believe us then. We would carry out our plan as soon as Trey went to sleep that night, which would be early since he had begun taking Xanax for his nerves.

Around eight o'clock that night, Trey took his medicine and laid down on the sofa. He watched television to clear his mind for about a half hour when I noticed he was fighting to hold his eyes open. I glanced over at Heather, who was sitting in the recliner across from us, and she gave her head a quick tilt to confirm the plan was set.

The second we heard Trey snore, we sprang into action. Heather called the police and told them to come quick, reporting that someone was trying to break into our home. Even though that was a lie, we believed it would force officers to rush right over. As soon as she hung up the phone, we quietly slipped through the front door and made a break for my car. I was nervous to start my engine for fear that it might wake Trey up. Thankfully, we were able to get it started and make our way down the driveway without disturbing him.

As we approached the bottom of the driveway, Heather pulled her cellphone out and had begun to film when she was stunned by something. Her eyes grew twice their size, and there was a tremble in her lips.

"What? What is it?" I asked.

She kept quiet. I followed her eyes to the neighbors' porch, where I immediately recognized another face. Right beside Officer Taylor sat a stalky man with dark hair.

"Dakota!" I gasped.

Heather slowly lowered the phone. Her jaw fell open as her eyes filled with tears. She was both speechless and disturbed.

When I noticed his eyes were shut, I became suspicious. I knew it was just too good to be true — that wasn't the same

Dakota Heather and I knew sitting there.

Heather made a grab for the door handle, and I tried my best to hold her back. I knew she would discover him to be in the same condition as Officer Taylor, and I wasn't too sure she could handle that. In that moment, her heart got the best of her, and there was nothing I could do to keep her seated in the vehicle with me.

She forcefully pushed me away and dashed out of the car. As she gradually stepped closer to him, I cut my high beams on so that we could see better before stepping out of the vehicle to follow her.

"Dakota?" said Heather with a shaky voice. She carefully made her way across the narrow dirt road toward him.

When he didn't respond to her, I knew my suspicion was right—that wasn't Dakota sitting on that porch. It was his body, but not his mind. I gave my best attempt at trying to convince her to step back and return to the vehicle, but she couldn't turn around and leave without him.

"Baby, it's me," she stressed as we continued stepping closer to him.

The way he sat there with his eyes closed as if he didn't recognize her voice was soul-crushing.

"Let's just go get Trey and wait for the police," I whispered hastily to her.

Nothing could break her focus away from him. Determined to get his attention, she completely ignored my request and continued walking toward him. Glued to her side, I couldn't let her approach him alone.

"Dakota," she continued. "Baby, come on, let's get you

out of here."

As Heather made her way into their yard, Dakota stood up, along with Officer Taylor and the young man. The three of them let out a chilling whisper.

"Shh...don't speak! Shh...don't speak!"

Tears started flowing down Heather's face. She stepped up onto the porch where Dakota stood. "Oh no, baby, what have they done to you?"

The lump in my throat wouldn't allow me to take another step toward that porch. I couldn't bear to see Dakota in that state, so I stood back and tried to control my tears.

Heather made her way to the porch while the three of them continued whispering, "Shh...don't speak! Shh...don't speak!" Their mannerisms were nearly robotic, and I was certain at that point that they were drugged.

When Heather was finally close enough to him, she grabbed Dakota's arm and tried pulling him toward her, but he wouldn't budge. Instead, he remained perfectly still and continued whispering.

"Let's go!" Heather cried. "Please, baby! You have to come with me right now."

It was clear by then that Dakota wasn't going to move from that porch, and nothing we could possibly do would break his trance. Whatever drug Roberson had given him made him unable to recognize our voices.

"Snap out of it!" Heather demanded as she grew determined to wake him up. "Open your eyes and look at me!" Nothing seemed to get a reaction from him until Heather lost control and smacked him across the face. "Wake up!"

His head was forced sideways from the impact of her strike, but he continued whispering like nothing had happened, "Shh...don't speak!" When he slowly turned his head straight, Heather let out a haunting scream, and I dropped to my knees when we saw his face. His eyelids were open, revealing two black holes. Someone had removed the eyes from his skull.

"What have you done? What the fuck did you do to him?" Heather frantically yelled out as she smacked the young man standing near Dakota and beat against his torso.

"Heather!" I panicked as I stood to my feet. "We have to go, now!"

Heather couldn't regain control of her emotional outburst fast enough. The front door swung open, and out stepped Roberson. I was crippled by fear when I noticed the hedge clippers in his hand and Heather standing on the porch with him.

"Heather!" I screamed to gain her attention. It was too late. Roberson drew back and struck her with his fist, knocking her down onto the porch.

"Leave her alone!" I shrieked.

Unfortunately, my cries weren't enough to save her. All I could do was stand there in shock and scream as Roberson forced her mouth open. He jabbed the hedge clippers inside of her mouth, holding her throat with his free hand. I screamed for Dakota to help her, but nothing could break his trance. The young man removed a flashlight from his pocket and flashed it in my face as I stood there in shock.

"Help her, please help her!" I continued shouting, hoping

something would snap Dakota or Officer Taylor out of it.

All I could do was watch helplessly as Heather screamed for mercy. She tried fighting off Roberson, but she was no match against him. He glanced up at me with a devilish grin stretched upon his wicked face and forced the hedge clippers shut. I felt faint as blood rushed down Heather's cheeks and started to slowly form a puddle on the porch where she lay, helpless.

Knowing I had just witnessed my friend getting her tongue cut out, I wailed. I frantically stumbled toward my car. I knew I had to get out of there if I wanted to keep my eyes and tongue intact, but my vision was so blurry from the adrenaline I couldn't tell left from right. I followed the faint white lights coming from my car until I managed to make my way back to it.

Heather's screams were assaulting my ears as I regained my consciousness and climbed into my car. I was no match for Roberson alone, and as much as I regretted leaving Heather, I had no choice. I punched the gas and headed up the driveway, spinning wheels. I whipped into the backyard and ran as fast as I could into the house, screaming in panic.

After rushing to the sofa, I started compulsively shaking Trey to awaken him. I had always known Roberson was dangerous, but I had no idea he was capable of such insanity. The only thing I could think about at that moment was waking up Trey and getting the hell out of there.

"Trey! Trey, wake up!" I cried. Trey slowly opened his eyes in a distraught manner. "He cut her tongue out! He cut Heather's tongue out!" I bawled.

"What? Calm down. What's going on?" Trey quickly sat up and grabbed my hand.

"We have to go!" I exclaimed. "We have to go right now!"

Trey appeared confused and completely thrown off by my cries. "Leah, you have to calm down. What's going on?"

"Roberson! We called the police and went down there to take a picture of them. And...and—" I couldn't think clearly enough to form a complete sentence.

"Wait," Trey interrupted. "Slow down. You called the police?" He asked as he tried to make sense of what I was saying.

"Yes!" I frantically exclaimed. "We thought if we took a picture of Officer Taylor and showed the police, they'd believe us. Instead, we saw Dakota, and his eyes are gone!" I cried, waving my hands erratically. "Roberson cut his eyes out, and now he is mutilating Heather. He's going to kill us if we don't get out of here right now!"

Trey finally received my message loud and clear. He shot up from the sofa and let out a forceful breath. "O-okay, let's go."

We made a break for the back door, but as soon as we opened it, there stood Roberson, holding the hedge clippers covered in blood. As we stood face to face with him, I couldn't help but notice the look of insanity spread upon his face. His nostrils were flared, yet he stood there, grinning with a glare that pierced through my soul.

I screamed out in terror as Trey slammed the door shut and grabbed my hand. He pulled me toward his side, and we expeditiously made our way toward the front door. Once

141

we approached the only other exit in the house, we both fell speechless when we saw the young man standing on the other side of the storm door with his eyes closed. There was no way out without risking our safety.

"We need to hide," Trey whispered.

A loud squeak informed us that the back door was opening.

We darted to Heather and Dakota's room and dove under their king-sized bed. I knew the police were on the way, so if we could just wait it out long enough, we would be saved.

The two of us lie under the bed, perfectly still, as the sound of footsteps tapped against the wooden floors through the house. We had a clear view of the bottom of the bedroom door where we stared fixedly, hoping no one would come walking in. I could feel Trey's pulse racing through his arm, which was pressed tightly against mine. I covered my mouth, desperate to keep my heavy breathing from being heard. Completely terrified, all we could do was listen as the footsteps came closer to the room we were hiding in. Was this it? Would this be the moment where my life would be ripped from me? We had to remain perfectly still and totally quiet if we were going to survive. All I could do was pray Roberson wouldn't think to check under the bed.

My heart nearly jumped out of my chest when I saw the bedroom door swing open. Two black boots emerged into view as someone stepped into the room. We watched helplessly as the boots tapped around the bed. Trey gently glanced toward me and motioned for me to remain completely still. Just as I started to see my life flash before my eyes, I heard a voice.

"Hello? Police. Is anyone home?"

It was a police officer! I glanced over at Trey and noticed a look of instant relief come over his face. He let out a deep breath and bowed his head briefly.

I inched my way toward the edge of the bed frame. Just as I started to call out to the officer to let him know we were there, Trey jerked me back, quickly covering my mouth, and pointed toward the door. I directed my attention back toward the base of the door, where I saw two dark brown boots come stepping in. Judging by the dirt covering these boots, I knew it wasn't another police officer.

As the second pair of boots quietly entered the room, the officer turned around and yelled, "Stop right there!"

The brown pair of boot stormed toward him. The two grappled for a second until an ear piercing scream echoed through the room. I bit down onto the palm of my hand as tears fell down my cheeks. The sounds of gagging and flesh ripping told me that something terrible was happening to the officer. Trey and I were forced to slowly inch back when a puddle of blood began to spread toward us on the bedroom floor.

The officer's body fell to the ground, and his head rolled toward us. It took everything I had not to scream when I noticed the officer's eyes had been cut from his head. His hand twitched lifelessly as the blood oozed from his face. It felt like the empty holes where eyes once sat were staring right at me in a dead silence.

I continued to bite into my palm to keep my emotions contained as we watched the dirty brown boots pace around

143

the room.

Roberson searched the room for Trey and me. "I like it when people hide—it makes things much more interesting for me." He was a very deranged man that seemed to enjoy hunting for us. "You thought the five-o would help you? Don't you get it by now?"

I didn't know what he meant by that remark, and at the moment, I didn't care. My only concern was getting out of there alive.

Trey and I kept quiet, barely breathing, and listened to him. He chuckled like a mad man. "Don't you two want to join your friends? It won't hurt too bad. And boy, I'll be sure your turn is first so you won't have to see a thing happen to your little girlfriend."

Once we heard the closet door swing open, it became clear to us that Roberson knew we were in that bedroom, and he wasn't going to stop looking until he found us. I thought about making a run for it, but there was no way we could move quickly enough to slide out from under the bed and make it past Roberson.

When we heard his footsteps enter the bathroom connected to Heather and Dakota's bedroom, Trey slowly reached into his pocket. I wasn't sure what his plan was, but I trusted he had schemed up something. I watched nervously as he slowly started pulling his car keys out, being cautious to keep them from jingling. Once he managed to successfully remove his keys from his pocket, he pushed the panic button on his key chain, causing his obnoxious alarm system to sound off.

The raucous beeping and whistling rippled through the

air, grabbing Roberson's focus. The brown boots hurtled out the room toward the commotion.

"Come on!" Trey demanded the moment Roberson departed.

He shoved the officer's lifeless body out of the way and crawled out from under the bed. I inched forward, following him. He snatched Dakota's gun from inside of the nightstand beside their bed and shoved it into his back pocket.

Trey grabbed my hand and held it tightly. "We have to make a break for your car," he declared with beads of sweat falling down his brow. While Roberson was distracted with the alarm system in Trey's car, which was parked in the driveway, we had a golden opportunity to make a run for my vehicle, parked in the back yard. I stepped over the officer's body, being careful to avoid slipping in his blood and followed Trey out of the bedroom.

As we rounded the corner into the kitchen, where the back door was located, we ran right into the young man. His head was slightly tilted, and his eyes were closed.

Shocked by his sudden appearance, I impulsively screamed.

He held his index finger against his lips and whispered, "Shh...don't speak!" Then he pointed toward the back door, almost like he was trying to help us by pointing us in the direction we needed to run.

Trey shoved his way past and yelled for me to come on. The two of us ran out the back door and jumped into my car, locking the doors behind us.

"Hurry! Drive! Just drive!" Trey panicked.

145

I struggled getting the key into the ignition, but once I finally did, I punched the car into reverse, turned the steering wheel sharply, and sped around before shifting it back into drive. Gravel slung in all directions as we flew down the driveway. I didn't see Roberson anywhere in our yard, but I also didn't look very hard. The only thing on my mind at that moment was getting as far away from there as possible.

As we drew nearer to the bottom of the driveway, Trey yelled out, "Nails! Look out, there's nails in the road!" Thank God for his sharp eye. Lines of nails were set up across the road, blocking us from exiting. I slammed on the brakes, creating a loud screeching sound from the burning rubber on my tires.

"Stay right here!" Trey demanded. "I'll move them."

"No! You aren't leaving this car!" I frantically yelled out.

Trey stepped out of the car. "We have to move them. I'll be quick; just keep a lookout." He glanced around to make sure Roberson wasn't nearby and swiftly started kicking the nails out of our path.

"Hurry up!" I panicked as I looked around to keep guard. It was a dark, sinister night, so it was next to impossible to see anything that wasn't directly in front of my headlights. I watched Trey continue kicking the nails out of our range when I noticed a shadow growing behind him. As the shadow continued to grow bigger, it registered in my brain that something was approaching Trey. I glanced over and noticed a large figure stepping out of the woods next to the driveway. There was only one person that could cast a shadow so large — Roberson!

"Trey! Trey! Look out!"

My heart sank as Roberson stepped in front of my headlights, holding the bloody hedge clippers. Trey pulled Dakota's gun out from the back of his pants, and without hesitating, he fired a shot directly at Roberson. Trey slowly stepped back when he realized the bullet didn't seem to faze Roberson. He rapidly fired another shot, and there was no doubt that the bullet penetrated Roberson that time.

Roberson's demented laugh spread through the thick air as he continued to make his way toward Trey. No matter how many rounds Trey emptied into his flesh, Roberson just kept coming closer.

"Leave us alone!" I roared.

Once he inched his way close enough, Roberson grabbed Trey by the throat and started strangling him with one hand while he held up the hedge clippers with the other. He slammed Trey, back first, onto the road and planted his knees on top of his chest.

Trey fought to push Roberson's arms back once he saw the hedge clippers moving toward his face.

"Stop! Stop it!" I screamed out in agony.

Trey attempted to fight him off, but he just wasn't physically powerful enough to stop Roberson.

"Just go!" Trey ordered. "Get out of here, Leah!"

"No! I won't leave you." I cried. I begged Roberson for mercy. "Please! Please let him go. We will leave, and we will never come back, I swear to you!"

To my dismay, this only made Roberson chuckle louder. "Your turn's next." He glared toward me, grinning devilishly.

"Go, Leah! Just get out of here!" Trey demanded once more.

Trey's arms buckled under Roberson's strength. The sharp blade of the hedge clippers jabbed downward into Trey's eye.

"No! Please!" I shrieked.

Roberson pushed against the handle of the blade, wedging the hedge clippers deep into Trey's flesh.

My heart palpitated, and the world around me slowed down for a moment. I watched helplessly as the blood ran down my lover's face. The way Trey screamed out in pain will forever haunt me. There was nothing more I could do at that moment but drive off in a desperate attempt to save myself. Through my tears, I could see Heather sitting beside the little girl on that porch. Knowing she was now one of them, just as Trey was about to be, all I could do was speed away, sobbing uncontrollably. I punched the gas and didn't stop until I arrived at the police station.

"So tell me, Sheriff, are you just another asshole in a uniform that will ignore my pleas? Or do you plan to help me?"

CHAPTER 11

LET IT BURN

The sheriff appeared to be filled with disquietude as he finished writing down my statement. As troubling as the events may have sounded, he couldn't have imagined what it was like to live through that hell. My best friends were mutilated, and I'd watched helplessly as the man I loved pleaded for his life before I left him there alone to suffer. What made it worse was the fact that we had reached out for help so many times, yet no one had done a thing for us.

After reliving my nightmare, my hands no longer trembled in fear. Instead, I found myself feeling hungry for answers and justice. A sense of fury pumped through my body as I revisited the scenes I had witnessed. Roberson needed to pay for what he did to Trey, Heather, and Dakota, and I wouldn't rest until he did.

"I have officers searching the entire premises and detectives working to find out who owns the property. We will get to the bottom of this, Leah, I assure you."

I couldn't help but think of all the times I had heard

those words before. Roberson was immune to the police and always managed to fly beneath their radar. Besides, why were detectives just now conducting in-depth searches? Why did all of this have to happen to me in order for my cries to be taken seriously? The answers to those questions really didn't matter. Nothing was going to undo the damage that had been done.

A faint knocking sound at the door interrupted our conversation. "Come in," the sheriff said.

A chubby man with rosy red cheeks entered the room, holding documents in one hand and was nervously straightening his tie with the other.

"Sir," the man started while completely ignoring me and focusing his attention toward the sheriff. "Can I have a quick word with you in private?"

"Yeah, sure," the sheriff responded. He glanced at me, almost like he needed my permission. The two of them stepped out of the room, closing the door behind them.

I watched the hour hand on the clock switch over to five-o-clock in the morning as I sat there listening to their whispers on the other side of the door. I couldn't make out what they were discussing but wondered if it was something related to my situation. I waited anxiously for the sheriff to finish his conversation, biting my fingernails down to nothing. I wanted to keep my mind off of Trey as much as possible. Every time I thought of him, all I could see was that scared look on his face. I had abandoned him, and the guilt had already started to sink in. Even though there was very little I could've done to stop Roberson, I should've at least tried.

My thoughts were interrupted when the door slowly screeched open. I heard the sheriff say, "Go ahead and have a chat with her." I assumed he was talking about me when the two of them came marching back in, and the chubby man took the only other available seat at the table across from me.

As the sheriff stood against the wall next to me with his arms crossed, the chubby man introduced himself. "Hi Leah, I'm Detective Flint." He fiddled with the documents in his hand.

I didn't intend on making new friends or meeting new people. My only concern at the moment was catching Roberson. "Have you found him?" I eagerly questioned.

Detective Flint glanced over at the sheriff as if the two of them were sharing some sort of secret I had yet to be let in on.

"Well?" I asked.

The detective cleared his throat awkwardly. "Leah, sometimes, when we go through something traumatic, we use self-defense mechanisms to protect us. This can cause us to distort reality sometimes."

I glared at him, trying to uncover what he was getting at. "What the hell is that supposed to mean?" I asked. I already knew he was trying to accuse me of lying about my statement, which was more mind-numbing than it was upsetting.

He took a deep breath and went on to explain. "What you went through tonight was very horrifying, I'm sure. Maybe you are making up details that didn't really happen?"

I chuckled sarcastically and shook my head in disbelief. "I know what happened!" I exclaimed. "You need to do your job and catch the man that has my friends and boyfriend!" I couldn't believe he was seriously considering the idea that I was making up details. After everything I had been through and explained to the sheriff, I expected to be treated with more respect and sympathy.

Detective Flint took another deep breath and turned to look at the sheriff. The sheriff nodded his head at the detective, signaling for him to carry on. Detective Flint repositioned himself, sitting up perfectly straight as he focused in on me. "Leah, there is no easy way to say this. Just take a look at this." He pulled one of the documents out and slid it on the table toward me.

It was an old black and white picture of Roberson, the old woman, and the young man. As I started studying the picture, I immediately noticed that the lady and her baby, as well as the little girl, were missing from the photo. I also noticed how much younger they looked. The three of them had the same blank look in their eyes and appeared to be drained of all emotion, except for the young man. There was something different about him in this picture. His eyes were open.

"Are they the people you are talking about?" He asked.

"That's them!" I said anxiously, pressing my index finger against Roberson's face in the photo. "That's Roberson! That is the monster you need to be out there trying to catch."

The detective gazed at me in disbelief. "I have an article I believe you need to read."

At that point, the sheriff spoke up. "That's enough. She has been through enough tonight." He rushed over and removed the documents from the detective's hand. This made my curiosity spiral. I wondered what was written on those documents.

"No. I would like to see whatever it is," I declared.

The sheriff appeared to be hesitant as the detective insisted it was in my best interest to see them.

Once I had the documents in my hands, I started skimming through them. The first one was an old newspaper clipping with the headline reading, Woman and Child go Missing. I started scanning the article. "Thirty-six-year-old Angie Norway and her three-month-old baby girl, Ariel Norway, went missing May 12, 1989." I continued scouring the article and discovered the two of them had been living in the same house that Trey, Dakota, Heather, and I were renting. "Police report many disturbances from Ms. Norway, who claimed her neighbors were harassing her. Upon multiple inspections, authorities report there were no neighbors anywhere near Ms. Norway's property...."

I stopped reading when I noticed a small black and white picture attached to the newspaper clipping. It was the middle-aged lady and her baby I had seen every day sitting on the neighbors' porch! How could this be? How did she still look the exact same after twenty-nine years? And how had her baby not aged? Surely by then, that baby should no longer need to be bundled up in a pink blanket and rocked on someone's lap. The child should have been older than me by now.

I tossed the article aside and snatched the next newspaper clipping. The headline read, Missing Child, and there was a picture of the little girl I had seen so many times sitting on that porch, dressed in the same cut off denim shorts and purple shirt. I briefly read over the article until I discovered the child had also gone missing from the same house Trey, Dakota, Heather, and I were renting. The trembling in my hands returned as I tossed the article aside and flipped to the final document.

It was an old newspaper clipping with a black and white picture of Roberson on the front cover. The title read, 1952 Massacre. The article was long, and I was slightly hesitant to read it, but I knew I had to. I needed answers, and these newspaper articles were the only documents I had stumbled across that had any information at all related to Roberson. If I wanted to stop Roberson and make him pay for what he did, I needed to read this.

I took a deep breath and started scanning the article.

Pictured above is forty-eight-year-old William Roberson, or as the local folk called him, Roberson. Over the years, Roberson has been associated with a few deaths, but perhaps none as shocking as the massacre on the night of Saturday, June 17, 1952.

Roberson worked at a local tire shop in Rockwood. Those that worked with him say he was a deranged man. Fellow employees shared with authorities how intimidating Roberson's nature was and how enraged he would become over minor issues. Local mechanic John Becker was decapitated when a machine malfunctioned, causing a car to fall on top of him. Roberson, being the only other worker present, was fired after the incident.

The few local folks that knew him outside of work believe

Roberson became furious over the loss of his job and often took his rage out on his only son, nineteen-year-old David Roberson, and his mother, seventy-nine-year-old Debra Roberson. According to locals, Roberson did not like noise of any kind and made it well known. The community of Rockwood knew not to make a wrong turn onto Roberson's street because he would lay nails in the road in order to pop their tires. According to his record, there were quite a few reports against him for destruction of property and the use of threatening language. Roberson used these tactics to keep people away from his property so that he wouldn't have to hear anyone or anything.

Reports from the local pub, where Roberson would often spend his weekends drinking, stated he completely lost his mind when he discovered the news that a house was going to be placed across the street from him. A real estate company purchased the property and planned to fix up the land and rent it out. Roberson made threats toward city council members and the mayor to stop the house from being built near him. When asked why he was so against the house being built, his response was, "I can't have anyone near me, especially a bitch. Women talk too much, and I can't stand noise."

Rockwood High School, where David Roberson was a student, released a statement, telling authorities that David often came to school with black eyes and bruises. Teachers confessed they were too scared of Roberson to report the abuse to authorities. They feared what Roberson might do to them if he discovered they turned him in. Fellow students claim David informed them of his father's strong distaste of noise.

A few peers of David's claimed he confessed to them that his father cut his grandmother's tongue out as punishment and to keep her from ever speaking again.

Once the house was finally constructed near Roberson's property, the Madison family moved in. They filed many reports, ranging from lights shining through their windows to people standing in their yard. Shortly before the Madison family decided to move due to the constant harassment they endured, they made one last police report.

On the night of Saturday, June 17th, police received a disturbance call from Greg Madison, Roberson's neighbor. He reported loud screams coming from Roberson's home. What the officers discovered at the scene was the goriest massacre, the community of Rockwood had seen. Roberson had butchered his mother and cut his son's eyes out. Debra Roberson was dead on arrival, and authorities reported a feeling of discomfort when they discovered her tongue had been removed. David Roberson was still alive, but his condition was critical. Authorities found Roberson in the back yard laughing hysterically before he took his own life with a shotgun. Local police state it was the bloodiest crime scene they had ever worked.

Before David Roberson passed away from his injuries three days later, he was able to release a few statements to the police. He reported that his father had a strong belief that men were superior to women. Roberson did not believe a woman should be allowed to speak out of turn, and if she did, she must be punished. Detectives asked David why his father cut his eyes out, to which David responded, "I was using them to protect women." He informed authorities that his father didn't like noise, so instead of talking, he would use lights to communicate to his grandmother and the neighbors when his father was in a bad mood. "One long flash meant you better not make a sound," David stated. He said this worked well for his grandmother and himself until the neighbors moved in. "They were always so loud," David told authorities. "I tried to warn them, but they wouldn't listen." Roberson caught David in the act of warning the neighbors by shining a flashlight toward their home. He claimed David was too weak to watch what needed to be done before removing his son's eyes. When Debra tried to help her grandson, Roberson killed her...."

I stopped reading and slid the documents away. I didn't know how to feel, confused, stunned, disbelieving. Detective Flint and the sheriff were both staring at me, waiting for me to say something. "This can't be true," I stated. I saw these people every day sitting on that front porch—there was no way they were all dead.

"Leah, it is true. No one has occupied that house since the deaths of Debra and David. There is no way you saw that man—he has been dead for many years," the sheriff declared.

I sat in silence, processing everything. The spotlight never cut on when the neighbors were in our yard. They were able to get inside of our vehicles even when the doors were locked. The police couldn't see them. I finally knew how they managed to do it all; they were ghosts. I thought about the little boy's words from the lake. "There's a monster with you." Cold chills shot through my skin, and my mind became flooded with new questions and answers to existing ones. Was Roberson following us the entire time? I now knew David, the young man, was the one shining the headlights every night. The entire time he was just trying to warn us because he knew what his father was going to do.

I couldn't hold back my tears as Trey, Dakota, and Heather entered my mind. The sheriff handed me a tissue. I sat there thinking about them being stuck there, on that porch, forever. They now belonged to Roberson and would forever haunt that property alongside Officer Taylor, the young man, the old woman, the middle-aged woman and her child, and the little girl. I couldn't bring justice for them, but I could make sure nobody else ever had to suffer the way that they had. I could also make sure that Roberson lived in Hell for eternity, where he belonged.

As the sun started to peep through the window blinds, I told Detective Flint and the sheriff that they were right. "Maybe I am making up details," I said. "I think I just need to go home and get a little rest."

Detective Flint nodded his head and gathered up the newspaper clippings.

"I think that's a good idea," the sheriff responded. "We can set you up with a hotel room for the next few days until we figure something out, and I'll assist you while you gather up your things."

"I'm fine," I responded. "The hotel room sounds great, but I can go get my things on my own."

On my way home, I stopped at a local store in town. Of

course, everyone stared at me, horrified since I was covered in blood and looked like I had just walked through the gates of Hell, but I didn't care. I purchased a dozen five-gallon gas cans and a book of matches, avoiding eye contact with everyone I passed. I made one last stop at a convenience store and filled each gas can up, then made a beeline straight to the house.

As I headed up the driveway, I didn't even take the time to look over at the neighbor's house. If Trey was sitting on that porch, I wasn't sure if I'd be able to stomach it. Instead, I kept my eyes fixed on the road and made my way up the hillside.

I stepped out of my car, leaving it running and grabbed six of the gas cans. Determined to make sure the landlord never rented that property to another family, I slung gasoline all through the house. I drenched the floors and covered the outer exterior. The rancid smell was eye-watering once I'd finished. I struck a match and dropped it to the ground, and watched as the flames spread like a virus, slowly engulfing the whole house. Dark smoke rolled through the yard, claiming every blade of grass that stood in its path.

I did what we should've done long ago, but there's no rewind button on this thing called life. Sometimes it takes extreme heartache to result in extreme measures. As soon as I knew nothing would be left once the flames burnt out, I got back in my car and made my way down the driveway.

The second I reached the bottom, I put my car in park and grabbed a gas can with each hand. I slung gasoline onto the neighbors' property, keeping my head pointed down—I didn't want to see Trey, Dakota, or Heather—it would just be too painful. I didn't stop slinging gasoline all over their property until the remaining six cans were empty. Tossing the empty containers into their yard and returning to my car, I turned the radio on and cranked the volume up as loud as it would go. I wanted Roberson to spend his final moments in that dry rotted shed he called home, surrounded by nothing but rambunctious noise.

The music blared through the air and the base vibrated against the road. I struck a match, and just as I was about to drop it onto the stream of gasoline leading toward the neighbors' property, I mistakenly glanced up. My heart sank into my stomach when I saw Trey sitting on their porch with his eyes shut. He looked peaceful, sitting next to Heather with his legs crossed. A part of me wanted to run to him and kiss him one last time, but the other part of me knew it was too late. A lump built in my throat when thoughts about the first time I'd seen him wandering the halls of Lincoln resurfaced. I knew that would be the last time I'd ever see his messy hair and sweet face.

The front door swung open, and Roberson stepped out onto the porch. I whispered, "Goodbye, my love," and gently blew a kiss toward Trey, and dropped the match to the ground. I got into my car, watching as the flames shot toward them. As the porch began to burn, one by one, everyone sitting there disappeared in the order they were killed. Once Officer Taylor vanished, I knew Dakota would leave next, followed by Heather, and then Trey. After they were all gone, leaving nothing but the burning shell of a house, I smiled through my tears and drove away. I couldn't save them, but I'd successfully set them free.

ABOUT THE AUTHOR

Rae Ann Carter is an aspiring writer with a passion for creating horror and suspense stories. She has been creating short stories since she was in elementary school and has won writing contests as early as her first-grade year. Born and raised in the historical city of Lexington, Virginia, she has worked as a volunteer with survivors of domestic violence. She has a strong educational background in psychology and graduated at the top of her class from Mary Baldwin University. In her free time, she enjoys photography, painting, and poetry.

Made in the USA
Columbia, SC
26 May 2023

17308312R00098